Artificial Condition

THE MURDERBOT DIARIES

ALSO BY MARTHA WELLS

THE MURDERBOT DIARIES
All Systems Red

BOOKS OF THE RAKSURA
The Cloud Roads
The Serpent Sea
The Siren Depths
The Edge of Worlds
The Harbors of the Sun
Stories of the Raksura: Volume I (short fiction)
Stories of the Raksura: Volume II (short fiction)

THE FALL OF ILE-RIEN TRILOGY
The Wizard Hunters
The Ships of Air
The Gate of Gods

STANDALONE ILE-RIEN BOOKS
The Element of Fire
The Death of the Necromancer
Between Worlds: the Collected Ile-Rien and Cineth Stories

YA NOVELS
Emilie and the Hollow World
Emilie and the Sky World
Blade Singer (with Aaron de Orive)

TIE-IN NOVELS
Stargate Atlantis: Reliquary
Stargate Atlantis: Entanglement
Star Wars: Razor's Edge

City of Bones
Wheel of the Infinite

ARTIFICIAL CONDITION

THE MURDERBOT DIARIES

MARTHA WELLS

A TOM DOHERTY ASSOCIATES BOOK

NEW YORK

This is a work of fiction. All of the characters, organizations, and events portrayed in this novella are either products of the author's imagination or are used fictitiously.

ARTIFICIAL CONDITION

Copyright © 2018 by Martha Wells

All rights reserved.

Edited by Lee Harris

A Tor.com Book
Published by Tom Doherty Associates
175 Fifth Avenue
New York, NY 10010

www.tor.com

Tor® is a registered trademark of Macmillan Publishing Group, LLC.

The Library of Congress Cataloging-in-Publication Data is available upon request.

ISBN 978-1-250-18692-8 (hardcover)
ISBN 978-1-250-18693-5 (ebook)

Our books may be purchased in bulk for promotional, educational, or business use. Please contact your local bookseller or the Macmillan Corporate and Premium Sales Department at 1-800-221-7945, extension 5442, or by email at MacmillanSpecialMarkets@macmillan.com.

First Edition: May 2018

20 19 18

Artificial Condition

Chapter One

SECUNITS DON'T CARE ABOUT the news. Even after I hacked my governor module and got access to the feeds, I never paid much attention to it. Partly because downloading the entertainment media was less likely to trigger any alarms that might be set up on satellite and station networks; political and economic news was carried on different levels, closer to the protected data exchanges. But mostly because the news was boring and I didn't care what humans were doing to each other as long as I didn't have to a) stop it or b) clean up after it.

But as I crossed the transit ring's mall, a recent newsburst from Station was in the air, bouncing from one public feed to another. I skimmed it but most of my attention was on getting through the crowd while pretending to be an ordinary augmented human, and not a terrifying murderbot. This involved not panicking when anybody accidentally made eye contact with me.

Fortunately, the humans and augmented humans were too busy trying to get wherever they were going or searching the feed for directions and transport schedules.

Three passenger transports had come through wormholes along with the bot-driven cargo transport I had hitched a ride on, and the big mall between the different embarkation zones was crowded. Besides the humans, there were bots of all different shapes and sizes, drones buzzing along above the crowd, and cargo moving on the overhead walkways. The security drones wouldn't be scanning for SecUnits unless they were specifically instructed, and nothing had tried to ping me so far, which was a relief.

I was off the company's inventory, but this was still the Corporation Rim, and I was still property.

Though I was feeling pretty great about how well I was doing so far, considering this was only the second transit ring I had been through. SecUnits were shipped to our contracts as cargo, and we never went through the parts of stations or transit rings that were meant for people. I'd had to leave my armor behind in the deployment center on Station, but in the crowd I was almost as anonymous as if I was still wearing it. (Yes, that is something I had to keep repeating to myself.) I was wearing gray and black work clothes, the long sleeves of the T-shirt and jacket, the pants and boots covering all my inorganic parts, and I was carrying a knapsack. Among the varied and colorful clothes, hair, skin, and interfaces of the crowd, I didn't stand out. The dataport in the back of my neck was visible but the design was too close to the interfaces augmented humans often had implanted to draw any suspicion. Also, nobody thinks a murderbot is going to be walking along the transit mall like a person.

Then in my skim of the news broadcast I hit an image. It was me.

I didn't stop in my tracks because I have a lot of practice in not physically reacting to things no matter how much they shock or horrify me. I may have lost control of my expression for a second; I was used to always wearing a helmet and keeping it opaqued whenever possible.

I passed a big archway that led to several different food service counters and stopped near the opening to a small business district. Anyone who saw me would assume I was scanning their sites in the feed, looking for information.

The image in the newsburst was of me standing in the lobby of the station hotel with Pin-Lee and Ratthi. The focus was on Pin-Lee, on her determined expression, the annoyed tilt of her eyebrows, and her sharp business clothes. Ratthi and I, in gray PreservationAux survey uniforms, were faded into the background. I was listed as "and bodyguard" in the image tags, which was a relief, but I was braced for the worst as I replayed the story.

Huh, the station I had thought of as The Station, the location of the company offices and the deployment center where I was usually stored, was actually called Port FreeCommerce. I didn't know that. (When I was there, I was mostly in a repair cubicle, a transport box, or in standby waiting for a contract.) The news narrator mentioned in passing how Dr. Mensah had bought the SecUnit who saved her. (That was clearly the heart-warming note to relieve the otherwise grim story with the high body count.) But the journalists weren't used to seeing SecUnits except in armor, or in a bloody pile of leftover pieces when things went wrong. They hadn't connected the idea of a purchased SecUnit with what they assumed was the generic augmented human person going into the hotel with Pin-Lee and Ratthi. That was good.

The weird part was that some of our security recordings had been released. My vantage point, as I searched the DeltFall habitat and found the bodies. Views from Gurathin's and Pin-Lee's helmet cameras, when they found Mensah and what was left of me after the explosion. I scanned through it quickly, making sure there weren't any good views of my human face.

The rest of the story was about how the company and DeltFall, plus Preservation and three other non-corporate political entities who had had citizens in DeltFall's habitat, were ganging up on GrayCris. There was also a multi-cornered solicitor-fight going on in which some of the entities who were allies in the investigation were fighting each other over financial responsibility, jurisdiction, and bond guarantees. I didn't know how humans could keep it all straight. There weren't many details about what had actually happened after PreservationAux had managed to signal the company rescue transport, but it was enough to hope that anybody looking for the SecUnit in question would assume I was with Mensah and the others. Mensah and the others, of course, knew different.

Then I checked the timestamp and saw the newsburst was old, published the cycle after I had left the station. It must have come through a wormhole with one of the faster passenger transports. That meant the official news channels might have more recent info by now.

Right. I told myself there was no way anybody on this transit ring would be looking for a rogue SecUnit. From the info available in the public feed, there were no deployment centers here for any bond or security companies. My contracts had always been on isolated installations or uninhabited survey planets, and I thought that was pretty much the norm. Even the shows and serials on the entertainment feeds never showed SecUnits contracted to guard offices or cargo warehouses or shipwrights, or any of the other businesses common to transit rings. And all the SecUnits in the media were always in armor, faceless and terrifying to humans.

I merged with the crowd and started down the mall again. I had to be careful going anywhere I might be scanned for weapons, which was all the facilities for purchasing transport, including the little trams that circled the ring. I can hack a weapons scanner, but security protocols suggested that at the passenger facilities there would be a lot of them to deal with the crowds and I could only do so many at once. Plus, I would have to hack the payment system, and that sounded like way more trouble than it was worth at the moment. It was a long walk to the part of the ring for the outgoing bot-driven transports, but it gave me time to tap the entertainment feed and download new media.

On the way to this transit ring, alone on my empty cargo transport, I had had a chance to do a lot of thinking about why I had left Mensah, and what I wanted. I know, it was a surprise to me, too. But even I knew I couldn't spend the rest of my lifespan alone riding cargo transports and consuming media, as attractive as it sounded.

I had a plan now. Or I would have a plan, once I got the answer to an important question.

To get that answer I needed to go somewhere, and there were two bot-driven transports leaving here in the next cycle that would take me there. The first was a cargo transport not unlike the one I had used to get here. It was leaving later, and was a better option, as I would have more time to get to it and talk it into letting me board. I could hack a transport if I tried, but I really preferred not to. Spending that much time with something that didn't want you there, or that you had hacked to make it think it wanted you there, just seemed creepy.

Maps and schedules were available in the feed, tied to all the main navigation points along the ring, so I was able to find my way down to the cargo loading area, wait for the shift change, and cut through to the embarkation zone. I had to hack an ID-screening system and some weapon-scanning drones on the level above the zone, and then got pinged by a bot guarding the entrance to the commercial area. I didn't hurt it, just broke through its wall in the feed and deleted out of its memory any record of the encounter with me.

(I was designed to interface with company SecSystems, to be basically an interactive component of one. The safeguards on this station weren't the company's proprietary tech, but it was close enough. Also, nobody is as paranoid as the company about protecting the data it collects and/or steals, so I was used to security systems that were a lot more robust than this.)

Once down on the access floor, I had to be extremely careful, as there was no reason for someone not working to be here, and while most of the work was being done by hauler bots, there were uniformed humans and augmented humans here, too. More than I had counted on.

A lot of humans congregated near the lock for my prospective transport. I checked the feed for alerts and found there had been an accident involving a hauler. Various parties were sorting out the damage and who was to blame. I could have waited until they cleared out, but I wanted to get off this ring and get moving. And honestly, my image in the newsburst had rattled me and I wanted to just sink into my media downloads for a while and pretend I didn't exist. To do that I had to be secure on a locked automated transport ready to leave the ring.

I checked the maps again for my second possibility. It was attached to a different dock, one marked for private, non-commercial traffic. If I moved fast, I could get there before it left.

The schedule had it designated as a long-range research vessel. That sounded like something that would have a crew and probably passengers, but the attached info said it was bot-driven and currently tasked with a cargo run that would stop at the destination I wanted. I had done a historical search in the feed for its movements and found it was owned by a university based on a planet in this system, which rented it out for cargo trips in between assignments to help pay for its upkeep. The trip to my destination would take twenty-one cycles, and I was really looking forward to the isolation.

Getting into the private docks from the commercial docks was easy. I got control of the security system long enough to tell it not to notice that I didn't have authorization, and walked through behind a group of passengers and crew members.

I found the research transport's dock, and pinged it through the comm port. It pinged back almost immediately. All the info I had managed to pull off the feed said it was prepared for an automated run, but just to be sure I sent a hail for attention from human crew. The answer came back a null, no one home.

I pinged the transport again and gave it the same offer I had given the first transport: hundreds of hours of media, serials, books, music, including some new shows I had just picked up on the way through the transit mall, in exchange for a ride. I told it I was a free bot, trying to get back to its human guardian. (The "free bot" thing is deceptive. Bots are considered citizens in some noncorporate political entities like Preservation, but they still have appointed human guardians. Constructs sometimes fall under the same category as bots, sometimes under the same category as deadly weapons. (FYI, that is not a good category to be in.)) This is why I had been a free agent among humans for less than seven cycles, including time spent alone on a cargo transport, and I already needed a vacation.

There was a pause, then the research transport sent an acceptance and opened the lock for me.

Chapter Two

I WAITED TO MAKE sure the lock cycled closed, and that there were no alarms from the ringside, then went down the access corridor. From the schematic available in the shipboard feed, the compartments the transport was using for cargo were normally modular lab space. With the labs sealed and removed to the university's dock storage, there was plenty of room for cargo. I pushed my condensed packet of media into the transport's feed for it to take whenever it wanted.

The rest of the space was the usual engineering, supply storage, cabins, medical, mess hall, with the addition of a larger recreation area and some teaching suites. There was blue and white padding on the furniture and it had all been cleaned recently, though it still had a trace of that dirty sock smell that seems to hang around all human habitations. It was quiet, except for the faint noise of the air system, and my boots weren't making any sound on the deck covering.

I didn't need supplies. My system is self-regulating; I don't need food, water, or to eliminate fluids or solids, and

I don't need much air. I could have lasted on the minimal life support that was all that was provided when no people were aboard, but the transport had upped it a little. I thought that was nice of it.

I wandered around, visually checking things out to see that it matched the schematic, and just making sure everything was okay. I did it, even knowing that patrolling was a habit I was going to have to get over. There were a lot of things I was going to have to get over.

When constructs were first developed, they were originally supposed to have a pre-sentient level of intelligence, like the dumber variety of bot. But you can't put something as dumb as a hauler bot in charge of security for anything without spending even more money for expensive company-employed human supervisors. So they made us smarter. The anxiety and depression were side effects.

In the deployment center, when I was standing there while Dr. Mensah explained why she didn't want to rent me as part of the bond guarantee agreement, she had called the increase in intelligence a "hellish compromise."

This ship was not my responsibility and there were no human clients aboard that I had to keep anything from hurting, or keep from hurting themselves, or keep from hurting each other. But this was a nice ship with surprisingly little security, and I wondered why the owners didn't leave a few humans aboard to keep an eye on it. Like most bot-driven transports, the schematics said there were drones onboard to make repairs, but still.

I kept patrolling until I felt the rumble and clunk through the deck that meant the ship had just decoupled itself from the ring and started to move. The tension that had kept me down to 96 percent capacity eased; a murderbot's life is stressful in general, but it would be a long time before I got used to moving through human spaces with no armor, no way to hide my face.

I found a crew meeting area below the control deck and planted myself in one of the padded chairs. Repair cubicles and transport boxes don't have padding, so traveling in comfort was still a novelty. I started sorting through the new media I'd downloaded on the transit ring. It had some entertainment channels that weren't available on the company's portion of Port FreeCommerce, and they included a lot of new dramas and action series.

I'd never really had long periods of unobserved free time before. The leisure to sort through everything and get it organized, and give it my full attention, without having to monitor multiple systems and the clients' feeds, was still something I was getting used to. Before this, I'd either been on duty, on call, or stuck in a cubicle on standby waiting to be activated for a contract.

I chose a new serial that looked interesting (the tags promised extragalactic exploration, action, and mysteries) and started the first episode. I was ready to settle in until it was time to think about what I was going to do when I got to my destination, something I intended to put off until the last possible moment. Then, through my feed, something said, *You were lucky*.

I sat up. It was so unexpected, I had an adrenaline release from my organic parts.

Transports don't talk in words, even through the feed. They use images and strings of data to alert you to problems, but they're not designed for conversation. I was okay with that, because I wasn't designed for conversation, either. I had shared my stored media with the first transport, and it had given me access to its comm and feed streams so I could make sure no one knew where I was, and that had been the extent of our interaction.

I poked cautiously through the feed, wondering if I'd been fooled. I had the ability to scan, but without drones my range was limited, and with all the shielding and equipment around me I couldn't pick up anything but background readings from the ship's systems. Whoever owned the ship wanted to allow for proprietary research;

the only security cameras were on the hatches, nothing in the crew areas. Or nothing I could access. But the presence in the feed was too big and diffuse for a human or augmented human, I could tell that much even through the feed walls protecting it. And it sounded like a bot. When humans speak in the feed, they have to subvocalize and their mental voice tends to sound like their physical voice. Even augmented humans with full interfaces do it.

Maybe it was trying to be friendly and was just awkward at communicating. I said aloud, "Why am I lucky?"

That no one realized what you were.

That was less than reassuring. I said, cautiously, "What do you think I am?" If it was hostile, I didn't have a lot of options. Transport bots don't have bodies, other than the ship. The equivalent of its brain would be above me, near the bridge where the human flight crew would be stationed. And it wasn't like I had anywhere to go; we were moving out from the ring and making leisurely progress toward the wormhole.

It said, *You're a rogue SecUnit, a bot/human construct, with a scrambled governor module.* It poked me through the feed and I flinched. It said, *Do not attempt to hack my systems,* and for .00001 of a second it dropped its wall.

It was enough time for me to get a vivid image of what I was dealing with. Part of its function was extragalactic astronomic analysis and now all that processing power sat idle while it hauled cargo, waiting for its next mission. It could have squashed me like a bug through the feed, pushed through my wall and other defenses and stripped my memory. Probably while also plotting its wormhole jump, estimating the nutrition needs of a full crew complement for the next 66,000 hours, performing multiple neural surgeries in the medical suite, and beating the captain at tavla. I had never directly interacted with anything this powerful before.

You made a mistake, Murderbot, a really bad mistake. How the hell was I supposed to know there were transports sentient enough to be mean? There were evil bots on the entertainment feed all the time, but that wasn't real, it was just a scary story, a fantasy.

I'd *thought* it was a fantasy.

I said, "Okay," shut down my feed, and huddled down into the chair.

I'm not normally afraid of things, the way humans are. I've been shot hundreds of times, so many times I stopped keeping count, so many times the company stopped keeping count. I've been chewed on by hostile fauna, run over by heavy machinery, tortured by clients for amusement, memory purged, etc., etc. But the inside of my head had been my own for +33,000 hours and I was used to it now. I wanted to keep me the way I was.

The transport didn't respond. I tried to come up with countermeasures for all the different ways it could hurt me and how I could hurt it back. It was more like a SecUnit than a bot, so much so I wondered if it was a construct, if there was cloned organic brain tissue buried in its systems somewhere. I'd never tried to hack another SecUnit. It might be safest to go into standby for the duration of the trip, and trigger myself to wake when we reached my destination. Though that would leave me vulnerable to its drones.

I watched seconds click by, waiting to see if it reacted. I was glad I had noted the lack of cameras and not bothered trying to hack into the ship's security system. I understood now why the humans felt it didn't need additional protection. A bot with this complete control over its environment and the initiative and freedom to act could repel any attempt to board.

It had opened the hatch for me. It wanted me here.

Uh-oh.

Then it said, *You can continue to play the media.*

I just huddled there warily.

It added, *Don't sulk.*

I was afraid, but that made me irritated enough to show it that what it was doing to me was not exactly new. I sent through the feed, *SecUnits don't sulk. That would trigger punishment from the governor module,* and attached some brief recordings from my memory of what exactly that felt like.

Seconds added up to a minute, then another, then three more. It doesn't sound like much to humans, but for a conversation between bots, or excuse me, between a bot/human construct and a bot, it was a long time.

Then it said, *I'm sorry I frightened you.*

Okay, well. If you think I trusted that apology, you don't know Murderbot. Most likely it was playing a game with me. I said, "I don't want anything from you. I just want to ride to your next destination." I'd explained that earlier, before it opened the hatch for me, but it was worth repeating.

I felt it withdraw back behind its wall. I waited, and let my circulatory system purge the fear-generated chemicals. More time crawled by, and I started to get bored. Sitting here like this was too much like waiting in a cubicle after I'd been activated, waiting for the new clients to take delivery, for the next boring contract. If it was going to destroy me, at least I could get some media in before that happened. I started the new show again, but I was still too upset to enjoy it, so I stopped it and started rewatching an old episode of *Rise and Fall of Sanctuary Moon*.

After three episodes, I was calmer and reluctantly beginning to see the transport's perspective. A SecUnit could cause it a lot of internal damage if it wasn't careful, and rogue SecUnits were not exactly known for lying low and avoiding trouble. I hadn't hurt the last transport I had taken a ride on, but it didn't know that. I didn't understand why it had let me aboard, if it really didn't want to hurt me. I wouldn't have trusted me, if I was a transport.

Maybe it was like me, and it had taken an opportunity because it was there, not because it knew what it wanted.

It was still an asshole, though.

Six episodes later I felt the transport in the feed again, lurking. I ignored it, though it had to know I knew it was there. In human terms, it was like trying to ignore someone large and breathing heavily while they watched your personal display surface over your shoulder. While leaning on you.

I watched seven more episodes of *Sanctuary Moon* with it hanging around my feed. Then it pinged me, like I somehow might not know it had been in my feed all this time, and sent me a request to go back to the new adventure show I had started to watch when it had interrupted me.

(It was called *Worldhoppers,* and was about freelance explorers who extended the wormhole and ring networks into uninhabited star systems. It looked very unrealistic and inaccurate, which was exactly what I liked.)

"I gave you a copy of all my media when I came aboard," I said. I wasn't going to talk to it through the feed like it was my client. "Did you even look at it?"

I examined it for viral malware and other hazards.

And fuck you, I thought, and went back to *Sanctuary Moon.*

Two minutes later it repeated the ping and the request. I said, "Watch it yourself."

I tried. I can process the media more easily through your filter.

That made me stop. I didn't understand the problem.

It explained, *When my crew plays media, I can't process the context. Human interactions and environments outside my hull are largely unfamiliar.*

Now I understood. It needed to read my reactions to the show to really understand what was happening. Humans used the feed in different ways than bots (and constructs) so when its crew played their media, their reactions didn't become part of the data.

I found it odd that the transport was less interested in *Sanctuary Moon,* which took place on a colony, than *Worldhoppers,* which was about the crew of a large exploration ship. You'd think it would be too much like work—I avoided serials about survey teams and mining installations—but maybe familiar things were easier for it.

I was tempted to say no. But if it needed me to watch the show it wanted, then it couldn't get angry and destroy my brain. Also, I wanted to watch the show, too.

"It's not realistic," I told it. "It's not supposed to be realistic. It's a story, not a documentary. If you complain about that, I'll stop watching."

I will refrain from complaint, it said. (Imagine that in the most sarcastic tone you can, and you'll have some idea of how it sounded.)

So we watched *Worldhoppers*. It didn't complain about the lack of realism. After three episodes, it got agitated whenever a minor character was killed. When a major character died in the twentieth episode I had to pause seven minutes while it sat there in the feed doing the bot equivalent of staring at a wall, pretending that it had to run diagnostics. Then four episodes later the character came back to life and it was so relieved we had to watch that episode three times before it would go on.

At the climax of one of the main story lines, the plot suggested the ship might be catastrophically damaged and members of the crew killed or injured, and the transport was afraid to watch it. (That's obviously not how it phrased it, but yeah, it was afraid to watch it.) I was feeling a lot more charitable toward it by that point so was willing to let it ease into the episode by watching one to two minutes at a time.

After it was over, it just sat there, not even pretending to do diagnostics. It sat there for a full ten minutes, which is a lot of processing time for a bot that sophisticated. Then it said, *Again, please.*

So I started the first episode again.

After two more run-throughs of *Worldhoppers*, it wanted to see every other show I had about humans in ships. Though after we encountered one based on a true story, where the ship experienced a hull breach and decompression killed several members of the crew (permanently, this time), it got too upset and I had to create a content filter. To give it a break, I suggested *Sanctuary Moon*. It agreed.

After four episodes, it asked me, *There are no SecUnits in this story?*

It must have thought that *Sanctuary Moon* was my favorite for the same reason that it liked *Worldhoppers*. I said, "No. There aren't that many shows with SecUnits, and they're either villains or the villain's minions." The only SecUnits in entertainment media were rogues, out to kill all humans because they forgot who built the repair cubicles, I guess. In some of the worst shows, SecUnits would sometimes have sex with the human characters. This was weirdly inaccurate and also anatomically complicated. Constructs with intercourse-related human parts are sexbots, not SecUnits. Sexbots don't have interior weapon systems, so it isn't like it's easy to confuse them with SecUnits. (SecUnits also have less than null interest in human or any other kind of sex, trust me on that.)

Granted, it would have been hard to show realistic SecUnits in visual media, which would involve depicting hours of standing around in brain-numbing boredom, while your nervous clients tried to pretend you weren't there. But there weren't any depictions of SecUnits in books, either. I guess you can't tell a story from the point of view of something that you don't think has a point of view.

It said, *The depiction is unrealistic.*

(You know, just imagine everything it says in the most sarcastic tone possible.)

"There's unrealistic that takes you away from reality and unrealistic that reminds you that everybody's afraid of you." In the entertainment feed, SecUnits were what the clients expected: heartless killing machines that could go rogue at any second, for no reason, despite the governor modules.

The transport thought that over for 1.6 seconds. In a less sarcastic tone, it said, *You dislike your function. I don't understand how that is possible.*

Its function was traveling through what it thought of as the endlessly fascinating sensation of space, and keeping all its human and otherwise passengers safe inside its metal body. Of course it didn't understand not wanting to perform your function. Its function was great.

"I like parts of my function." I liked protecting people and things. I liked figuring out smart ways to protect people and things. I liked being right.

Then why are you here? You are not a "free bot" looking for your guardian, who presumably cannot simply be sent a message via the public comm relay on the transit ring we recently departed.

The question caught me by surprise, because I hadn't thought it was interested in anything besides itself. I hesitated, but it already knew I was a SecUnit, and it already knew there was just no circumstance where it was legal and okay that I was here. It might as well know who I was. I sent my copy of the Port FreeCommerce newsburst into the feed. "That's me."

Dr. Mensah of PreservationAux purchased you and allowed you to leave?

"Yes. Do you want to watch *WorldHoppers* again?" I

regretted the question an instant later. It knew that was an attempt at a distraction.

But it said, *I am not allowed to accept unauthorized passengers or cargo, and have had to alter my log to hide any evidence of your presence.* There was a hesitation. *So we both have a secret.*

I had no reason not to tell it, except fear of sounding stupid. "I left without permission. She offered me a home with her on Preservation, but she doesn't need me there. They don't need SecUnits there. And I . . . didn't know what I wanted, if I wanted to go to Preservation or not. If I want a human guardian, which is just a different word for owner. I knew it would be easier to escape from the station than it would from a planet. So I left. Why did you let me onboard?"

I thought maybe I could distract it by getting it to talk about itself. Wrong again. It said, *I was curious about you, and cargo runs are tedious without passengers. You left to travel to RaviHyral Mining Facility Q Station. Why?*

"I left to get off Port FreeCommerce, away from the company." It waited. "After I had a chance to think, I decided to go to RaviHyral. I need to research something, and that's the best place to do it."

I thought the mention of research might stop its questions, since it understood research. No, not so much. *There were public library feeds available on the transit ring, with information exchange to the planetary archives. Why not do the research there? My onboard archives are extensive. Why haven't you sought access to them?*

I didn't answer. It waited thirty whole seconds, then it said, *The systems of constructs are inherently inferior to advanced bots, but you aren't stupid.*

Yeah, well, fuck you, too, I thought, and initiated a shutdown sequence.

Chapter Three

I JOLTED AWAKE FOUR hours later, when my automatic recharge cycle started. The transport said immediately, *That was unnecessarily childish.*

"What do you know about children?" I was even more angry now because it was right. The shutdown and the time I had spent inert would have driven off or distracted a human; the transport had just waited to resume the argument.

My crew complement includes teachers and students. I have accumulated many examples of childishness.

I just sat there, fuming. I wanted to go back to watching media, but I knew it would think it meant I was giving in, accepting the inevitable. For my entire existence, at least the parts I could remember, I had done nothing but accept the inevitable. I was tired of it.

We are friends now. I don't understand why you won't discuss your plans.

It was such an astonishing, infuriating statement. "We aren't friends. The first thing you did when we were underway was threaten me," I pointed out.

I needed to make certain you didn't attempt to harm me.

I noticed it had said "attempt" and not "intend." If it had cared anything about my intentions it wouldn't have let me onboard in the first place. It had enjoyed showing me it was more powerful than a SecUnit.

Not that it was wrong about the "attempt." While watching the episodes I had managed to do some analysis of it, using the schematics in its own public feed and the specs of similar transports available on the unsecured sections of its database. I had figured out twenty-seven different ways to render it inoperable and three to blow it up. But a mutually assured destruction scenario was not something I was interested in.

If I got through this intact, I needed to find a nicer, dumber transport for the next ride.

I hadn't responded and I knew by now it couldn't stand that. It said, *I apologized.* I still didn't respond. It added, *My crew always considers me trustworthy.*

I shouldn't have let it watch all those episodes of *Worldhoppers.* "I'm not your crew. I'm not a human. I'm a construct. Constructs and bots can't trust each other."

It was quiet for ten precious seconds, though I could tell from the spike in its feed activity it was doing something. I realized it must be searching its databases, looking for a way to refute my statement. Then it said, *Why not?*

I had spent so much time pretending to be patient with humans asking stupid questions. I should have more self-control than this. "Because we both have to follow human orders. A human could tell you to purge my memory. A human could tell me to destroy your systems."

I thought it would argue that I couldn't possibly hurt it, which would derail the whole conversation.

But it said, *There are no humans here now.*

I realized I had been trapped into this conversational dead end, with the transport pretending to need this explained in order to get me to articulate it to myself. I didn't know who I was more annoyed at, myself or it. No, I was definitely more annoyed at it.

I sat there for a while, wanting to go back to the media, any media, rather than think about this. I could feel it in the feed, waiting, watching me with all its attention except for the miniscule amount of awareness it needed to keep itself on course.

Did it really matter if it knew? Was I afraid knowing would change its opinion of me? (As far as I could tell, its opinion was already pretty low.) Did I really care what an asshole research transport thought about me?

I shouldn't have asked myself that question. I felt a wave of non-caring about to come over me, and I knew I couldn't let it. If I was going to follow my plan, such as it was, I needed to care. If I let myself not care, then there was no telling where I'd end up. Riding dumb transports watching media until somebody caught me and sold me back to the company, probably, or killed me for my inorganic parts.

I said, "At some point approximately 35,000 hours ago, I was assigned to a contract on RaviHyral Mining Facility Q Station. During that assignment, I went rogue and killed a large number of my clients. My memory of the incident was partially purged." SecUnit memory purges are always partial, due to the organic parts inside our heads. The purge can't wipe memory from organic neural tissue. "I need to know if the incident occurred due to a catastrophic failure of my governor module. That's what I think happened. But I need to know for sure." I hesitated, but what the hell, it already knew everything else. "I need to know if I hacked my governor module in order to cause the incident."

I don't know what I expected. I knew ART (aka Asshole Research Transport) had a deeper attachment to its crew than SecUnits had for clients. If it didn't feel that way about the humans it carried and worked with, then it wouldn't have gotten so upset whenever anything happened to the characters on *Worldhoppers*. I wouldn't have had to filter out all the based-on-a-true-story shows where human crews got hurt. I knew what it felt, because I felt that way about Mensah and PreservationAux.

It said, *Why was your memory of the incident purged?*

That wasn't the question I was expecting. "Because SecUnits are expensive and the company didn't want to lose any more money on me than it already had." I wanted to fidget. I wanted to say something so offensive to it that it would leave me alone. I really wanted to stop thinking about this and watch *Sanctuary Moon*. "Either I killed them due to a malfunction and then hacked the governor module, or I hacked the governor module so I could kill them," I said. "Those are the only two possibilities."

Are all constructs so illogical? said the Asshole Research Transport with the immense processing capability whose metaphorical hand I had had to hold because it had become emotionally compromised by a fictional media serial. Before I could say that, it added, *Those are not the first two possibilities to consider.*

I had no idea what it meant. "All right, what are the first two possibilities to consider?"

That it either happened, or it didn't.

I had to get up and pace.

Ignoring me, ART continued, *If it happened, did you cause it to happen, or did an outside influence use you to cause it to happen? If an outside influence caused it to happen, why? Who benefited from the incident?*

ART seemed happy to have the problem laid out so clearly. I wasn't sure I was. "I know I could have hacked my governor module." I pointed at my head. "Hacking my governor module is why I'm here."

If your ability to hack your governor module was what caused the incident, why was it not checked periodically and the current hack detected?

There would be no point in hacking the module if I couldn't fool the standard diagnostics. But . . . The company was cheap and sloppy, but not stupid. I had been kept in a deployment center attached to corporate offices. So they hadn't anticipated any potential danger.

ART said, *You are correct that further research is called for before the incident can be understood fully. How do you plan to proceed?*

I stopped pacing. It knew how I planned to proceed. Go to RaviHyral, look for information. There hadn't been anything in the company's knowledge base that I could access without getting caught, but the systems on RaviHyral itself might not be so well protected. And maybe if I saw the place again, it would spark something in my human neural tissue. (I wasn't much looking forward to that part, if it happened.) I could tell ART was doing that thing again where it asked me questions it knew the answer to so it could trap me into admitting stuff that I didn't want to admit. I decided to just skip to the end. "What do you mean?"

You will be identified as a SecUnit.

That stung a little. "I can pass as an augmented human." Augmented humans are still considered humans. I don't know if there are any augmented humans with enough implants to resemble a SecUnit. It seems unlikely a human would want that many implants, or would survive whatever catastrophic injury might make them necessary. But humans are weird. Whatever, I didn't intend to let anyone see more than I absolutely had to.

You look like a SecUnit. You move like a SecUnit. It sent a whole array of images into the feed, comparing a recording of me moving around its corridors and cabins with recordings of various members of its crew in the same spaces. I had relaxed, relieved to be off the transit ring, but I didn't look very relaxed. I looked like a patrolling SecUnit.

"No one noticed on the transit rings," I said. I knew I was taking a chance. I had gotten by so far because the humans and augmented humans in the commercial transport rings didn't see SecUnits except on the entertainment feed or in the news, where we were mostly killing people or already blasted into pieces. If I was spotted by anyone who had ever worked a long-term contract with SecUnits, there was a good chance they would realize what I was.

ART brought up a map listing. The RaviHyral Mining Facility Q Station was the third largest moon of a gas giant. The map rotated, with the various mining installations and support centers and the port highlighted. There was only the one port. *These installations will employ SecUnits/have employed SecUnits. You will be seen by human authorities who have worked with SecUnits.*

I hate it when ART is right. "I can't do anything about that."

You can't alter your configuration.

I could see the skepticism through the feed. "No, I can't. Look up the specs on SecUnits."

SecUnits are never altered. Skepticism intensifying. It had obviously pulled all the information on SecUnits in its database and assimilated it.

"No. Sexbots are altered." At least the ones I had seen had been altered. Some were mostly Unit standard with a few changes, others were radically different. "But that's done in the deployment center, in the repair cubicles. To do anything like that I'd need a medical suite. A full one, not just an emergency kit."

It said, *I have a full medical suite. Alterations can be made there.*

That was true, but even a medical suite as good as what

ART had, able to carry out thousands of unassisted procedures on humans, wouldn't have the programming to physically alter a SecUnit. I might be able to guide it through the process, but there was a big problem with that. Alterations to my organic and nonorganic components would cause catastrophic function loss if I wasn't deactivated when they took place. "Theoretically. But I can't operate the medical suite while I'm being altered."

I can.

I didn't say anything. I started sorting through my media again.

Why are you not responding?

I knew ART well enough by now to know it wouldn't leave me alone, so I went ahead and spelled it out. "You want me to trust you to alter my configuration while I'm inactive? When I'm helpless?"

It had the audacity to sound offended. *I assist my crew in many procedures.*

I got up, paced, stared at the bulkhead for two minutes, then ran a diagnostic. Finally, I said, "Why do you want to help me?"

I'm accustomed to assisting my crew with large-scale data analysis, and numerous other experiments. While I am in transport mode, I find my unused capacity tiresome. Solving your problems is an interesting exercise in lateral thinking.

"So you're bored? I'd be the best toy you've ever had?"

When I was on inventory, I would have given anything for twenty-one cycles of unobserved downtime. I couldn't feel sorry for ART. "If you're bored, watch the media I gave you."

I am aware that for you, your survival as a rogue Unit would be at stake.

I started to correct it, then stopped. Rogue was not how I thought of myself. I had hacked my governor module but continued to obey orders, at least most of them. I had not escaped from the company; Dr. Mensah had legally bought me. While I had left the hotel without her permission, she hadn't told me not to leave, either. (Yes, I know the last one isn't helping the argument all that much.)

Rogue units killed their human and augmented human clients. I . . . had done that once. But not voluntarily.

I needed to find out whether or not it had been voluntary.

"My survival isn't at stake if I continue to ride unoccupied transports." And learn to avoid the asshole ones that want to threaten me and question all my choices and try to talk me into getting into the medical suite so they could do experimental surgery on me.

Is that all you want? You don't want to return to your crew?

I said, not patiently, "I don't have a crew."

It sent me an image from the newsburst I had given it, a group image of PreservationAux. Everybody was in their gray uniforms, smiling, for a team portrait taken at the start of the contract. *That isn't your crew?*

I didn't know how to answer it.

I had spent thousands of hours watching or reading about, and liking, groups of fictional humans in the media. Then I had ended up with a group of real humans to watch and like, and then somebody tried to kill them, and while protecting them I had to tell them I had hacked my governor module. So I left. (Yes, I know it's more complicated than that.)

I tried to think about why I didn't want to change my configuration, even to help protect myself. Maybe because it was something humans did to sexbots. I was a murderbot, I had to have higher standards?

I didn't want to look more human than I already did. Even when I was still in armor, once my PreservationAux clients had seen my human face, they had wanted to treat me like a person. Make me ride in the crew section of the hopper, bring me in for their strategy meetings, talk to me. About my feelings. I couldn't take that.

But I didn't have the armor anymore. My appearance, my ability to pass as an augmented human, had to be my new armor. It wouldn't work if I couldn't pass among humans who were familiar with SecUnits.

But that seemed pointless, and I felt another wave of "I don't care" coming on. Why should I care? I liked humans, I liked watching them on the entertainment feed, where they couldn't interact with me. Where it was safe. For me and for them.

If I had gone back to Preservation with Dr. Mensah and the others, she might be able to guarantee my safety, but could I really guarantee her safety from me?

Altering my physical configuration still seemed drastic. But hacking my governor module was drastic. Leaving Dr. Mensah was drastic.

ART said, almost plaintively, *I don't understand why this is a difficult choice.*

I didn't, either, but I wasn't going to tell it that.

I took two cycles to think it over. I didn't talk to ART about it, or anything else, though we kept watching media together, and it exercised a self-restraint I didn't think it had and didn't try to start arguments with me.

I knew I had been lucky up to this point. Onboard the transport I had used to leave Port FreeCommerce, I had compared myself to recordings of humans, trying to isolate what factors might cause me to be identified as a SecUnit. The most correctable behavior was restless movement. Humans and augmented humans shift their weight when they stand, they react to sudden sounds and bright lights, they scratch themselves, they adjust their hair, they look in their pockets or bags to check for things that they already know are in there.

SecUnits don't move. Our default is to stand and stare at the things we're guarding. Partly this is because our non-organic parts don't need movement the way organic parts do. But mostly it's because we don't want to draw attention to ourselves. Any unusual movement might cause a human to think there's something wrong with you, which will draw more scrutiny. If you've gotten stuck with one of the bad contracts, it might cause the humans to order the HubSystem to use your governor module to immobilize you.

After analyzing human movement, I wrote some code for myself, to cause me to make a random series of movements periodically if I was standing still. To change my respiration to react to changes in the air quality. To vary my walking speed, to make sure I reacted to stimuli physically instead of just scanning and noting it. This code had gotten me through the second transit ring. But would I be all right on a ring or installation frequented by humans who often saw or worked with SecUnits?

I tweaked my code a little and asked ART to record me again as I moved around its corridors and compartments.

I tried to make myself look as much like a human as possible. I'm used to feeling mentally awkward around humans, and I took that sensation and tried to express it in my physical movements. I felt pretty good about the result. Until I looked at the recordings and compared them to ART's recordings of its crew and my recordings of other SecUnits.

The only one I was fooling here was myself.

The change in movement made me look more human but my proportions exactly matched the other SecUnits. I was good enough to fool humans who weren't looking for me, since humans tend to ignore non-standard behavior in transitional public spaces. But anyone who had set out to find me, who was alert to the possibility of a rogue SecUnit, might not be fooled, and a simple scan calibrated to search for SecUnit size, height, and weight was certain to find me.

It was the logical choice, it was the obvious choice, and I would still rather peel my human skin off than do it.

I was going to have to do it.

After a lot of argument, we agreed the easiest change for the best result was to take two centimeters of length out of my legs and arms. It doesn't sound like a big change, but it meant my physical proportions would no longer match Unit standard. It would change the way I walked, the way I moved. It made sense and I was fine with it.

Then ART said we also needed to change the code controlling my organic parts, so they could grow hair.

My first reaction to that was no fucking way. I had hair on my head, and eyebrows; that was a part of SecUnit configuration that was shared with sexbots, though the code controlling it kept SecUnit head hair short to keep it from interfering with the armor. The whole idea of constructs is that we look human, so we don't make the clients uncomfortable with our appearance. (I could have told the company that the fact that SecUnits are terrifying killing machines does, in fact, make humans nervous regardless of what we look like, but nobody listens to me.) But the rest of my skin was hairless.

I told ART that I preferred it that way and extra hair would just draw unwanted attention. It replied that it meant the fine, sparse hair humans had on parts of their skin. ART had done some analysis and come up with a list of biological features that humans might notice subliminally. Hair was the only one we could change my underlying code to create, and ART proposed that it would make the joins between the organic and inorganic parts on my arms, legs, chest, and back look more like augments, the inorganic parts that humans had implanted for medical or other reasons. I pointed out that many humans or augmented humans had the hair on their bodies removed, for hygienic or cosmetic reasons and because who the hell wants it there anyway. ART countered that humans didn't have to worry about being identified as SecUnits, so they could do whatever they wanted to their bodies.

I still wanted to argue, because I didn't want to agree with anything ART said right now. But it seemed minor in comparison to removing two centimeters of synthetic bone and metal from my legs and arms, and changing the code for how my organic parts would grow around them.

ART had an alternate, more drastic plan that included giving me sex-related parts, and I told it that was absolutely not an option. I didn't have any parts related to sex and I liked it that way. I had seen humans have sex on the entertainment feed and on my contracts, when I had been required to record everything the clients said and did. No, thank you, no. No.

But I did ask it to make an alteration to the dataport in the back of my neck. It was a vulnerable point, and I didn't want to miss the opportunity to take care of it.

Once we agreed on the process, I stood in front of the surgical suite. The MedSystem had just sterilized and prepped itself and there was a heavy scent of antibacterials in the air, reminding me of every time I had carried an injured client into a room like this. I was thinking about all the ways this could go wrong, and the terrible things ART could do to me if it wanted.

ART said, *What is causing the delay? Is there a preliminary process left to complete?*

I had no reason to trust it. Except the way it kept wanting to watch media about humans in ships, and got upset when the violence was too realistic.

I sighed, stripped off my clothes, and laid down on the surgical platform.

Chapter Four

I CAME BACK ONLINE to find I was at 26 percent capacity, but the percentage was climbing slowly. Bands of pain circled my knee and elbow joints, so intense I couldn't process it. My human skin itched. And I was leaking. I hate that.

I didn't have the capacity to access or play any of my media. All I could do was lie there waiting for my levels to adjust. Attempts to move just made it worse. I wished I had gone with Plan Sixteen to render the ART inoperable, the one with the best statistical chance of success without me taking catastrophic damage in retaliation. Plan Two to blow it up was looking pretty attractive at the moment, too. This had been a stupid thing to agree to.

It was like being in a cubicle after being shot to pieces, but without a cubicle's ability to shut down higher functions until the repairs were complete. I had known going in that the MedSystem wouldn't be able to adjust my pain level, but I hadn't thought it would be this bad. I couldn't adjust my own temperature, either, but I wasn't cold, as the MedSystem was controlling the temperature of the room and the platform to keep me at a comfortable level. Cubicles didn't do that and I had to admit it was nice.

Gradually my levels started to even out and I got back enough function to dial down my pain sensor and turn off the itching. I needed some pain to tell me what not to move until all the regrowth of my organic tissue was complete.

ART was hanging around out in my feed but mercifully hadn't tried to talk to me yet. At 75 percent capacity, I tried to sit up.

MedSystem started to throw warnings and ART said, *There is no reason to move now. During the process I ran a search of my onboard public information newsfeed bases during the time period in question, regarding unusual fatalities relating to mining. Do you want my conclusions based on the results?*

I eased back down, feeling my organic parts cling to the warm metal of the platform. I was now leaking from a different spot. I told ART I knew how to fucking read search results.

I would defer to your expertise in shooting and killing things. You should defer to mine in data analysis.

I told it fine, whatever. I didn't think there would be anything useful.

It sent its conclusions into the feed. Admittedly, it made sense that a large number of deaths under unusual circumstances would end up in some sort of public record available to multiple newsfeeds, the way the DeltFall incident had. The RaviHyral incident might have been classed as an accident, but a company bond was involved so there would have been a legal battle. Though if the data said it was a rogue SecUnit who had killed everyone, that didn't give me any more information than I already had.

Records across several archived newsfeeds indicate the site of the incident was likely a small installation called Ganaka Pit. The information originates in a source from Kalidon, a political entity on the Corporation Rim, where the company funding Ganaka Pit was based. There were fifty-seven fatalities. The cause is listed as "equipment failure."

SecUnits were categorized on inventory as equipment.

ART waited, and when I didn't say anything, added, *So your initial assumption was correct, the incident did occur. Investigation can now proceed.*

I wanted to shut down, but it would interfere with the healing process.

ART asked, *Do you wish to watch media?*

I didn't respond, but it started an episode of *Sanctuary Moon* anyway.

When I was finally able to climb off the platform, I fell on the deck, but by the end of that cycle I was almost back to normal. The first thing I did was wash off all the blood and other assorted fluids in the bathing facility attached to the MedSystem bay. Security ready rooms had facilities where I could clean off the blood and fluids after a fight or a repair, but I had never used a facility meant for humans. ART had good ones, with the recycled cleaning fluid that was so much like water it was hard to tell the difference without a chemical analysis. You could adjust the temperature to make it warmer, and it smelled good. I smelled like a clean human afterward, and that was just odd.

The fine hair that was coming up in patches in various places was strange but not as annoying as I had anticipated. It might be inconvenient the next time I had to put on a suit skin, but the humans with hair seemed to manage with a minimum of complaint, so I figured I would, too. The change in code had also made my eyebrows thicker and the hair on my head a few centimeters longer. I could feel it, and it was weird.

I went to ART's rec space and used the treadmill and the other machines to test myself, making sure my weapons were still functioning correctly and my aim wasn't off. (I didn't test fire them, as ART let me know that it would set off the fire protection system if I did.)

I looked at myself in the mirror for a long time.

I told myself I still looked like a SecUnit without armor, hopelessly exposed, but the truth was I did look more human. And now I knew why I hadn't wanted to do this.

It would make it harder for me to pretend not to be a person.

We exited the wormhole on schedule. As soon as we were in range of the transit ring, ART stretched its reception and picked up the destination info packet for me, which included a more detailed map of RaviHyral. Rotating the map to look at it from every angle didn't jog anything in the fragments of memory I had of that time. But it was interesting that Ganaka Pit wasn't marked anywhere.

I could feel ART in my feed, looking over my figurative shoulder again. I checked the timestamp, and saw the map had been updated multiple times since the time period of my incident. "They took it off the map."

Is this usual? ART asked. It dealt only with star maps, and removing something from one of those was kind of a big deal.

"I don't know if it's usual or not, but it makes sense, if the company or the clients wanted to conceal what happened." If the company wanted to continue to sell contracts for SecUnits to other mining installations, concealing the fact, or at least obscuring the fact, that fatalities had occurred was important. Maybe instead of a legal battle, the company had paid out on the bonds quickly under the condition that the client minimize details about the incident in the public record. This hadn't been a situation like GrayCris and DeltFall, where there were multiple parties involved and the company was all over the newsfeeds, trying to generate sympathy for itself.

ART pulled more historical info, searching the pit and service installation names that were listed. RaviHyral had originally been held by a number of companies with mining rights to different areas of the moon's interior. But over the past two system-years, a company called Umro had bought out some of the claims, though many of the original companies were still operating as contractors. None of the names sounded familiar.

I'd have to figure out where Ganaka Pit had been before I could go there. I would have been transported there as freight and there weren't any memories of the trip, partially erased or not.

I started to search through the rest of the info packet, looking for schedules. I would have to get a shuttle from the transit ring to the RaviHyral port. That would be tricky. Well, the whole thing would be tricky. From the information on the shipping schedule, only people with employment vouchers or passes from one of the mining installations or support services were allowed to board the shuttles. There was no tourism, nobody coming and going without official authorization from one of the companies or contractors on the moon. Since I wasn't a person and I didn't have an employment voucher, I would have to hack my way into one of the supply shuttles . . .

ART was still pulling data from the station feed. *I have a suggestion,* it told me, and displayed a set of personal advertisements. I had seen these in the feeds at Port FreeCommerce and the last transit ring, but hadn't paid attention. ART highlighted one that was a job listing for a temporary position as security for a technologist group on limited contract.

"What?" I asked ART. I didn't understand why it was showing me this.

If this group hired you, you would have an employment voucher for travel to the installation.

"Hire me." I've had more contracts than I can remember (I mean that literally. A lot of them were before the memory purge) but none of them were voluntary. The company pulled me out of storage, showed me to the client, then packed me into the cargo hold. "Have you lost your mind?"

My crew hires consultants for every voyage. ART was impatient that I wasn't complimenting it yet on its great idea. *The procedure is simple.*

"For humans and augmented humans, yes." I was stalling. I would have to interact with humans as an augmented human. I know that's what altering my configuration was supposed to be for, but I had imagined it as taking place from a distance, or in the spaces of a crowded transit ring. Interacting meant talking, and eye contact. I could already feel my performance capacity dropping.

It will be simple, ART insisted. *I'll assist you.*

Yes, the giant transport bot is going to help the construct SecUnit pretend to be human. This will go well.

Once ART was docked and the transit ring's bot-piloted tugs were removing the cargo modules, it cycled the lock for me and I slipped through into the embarkation zone.

It had given me access to its comm so it could ride my feed through the transit ring. It claimed it could help me and while I was skeptical of that, it could at least keep me company. As I walked away from the safety of ART's lock, I dropped back down to 96 percent efficiency. I hit the station entertainment feeds for new downloads to try to calm down.

I'd already sent a message to the social feed node about the advertisement, and gotten an answer with a location and timestamp. The last time I'd had an arranged meeting with humans they kidnapped Mensah and blew me up, so. This could hardly be worse.

I hacked my way through embarkation zone security and out into the ring's mall. It was utilitarian compared to both the last transit ring and Port FreeCommerce. No garden pods, no holo sculptures, no big holo displays advertising arrays of shipwrights and cargo factors and other businesses, no shiny new interface vending machines. Also no big passenger transports coming through, so not nearly as big a crowd, of humans or bots. ART's idea was beginning to seem less like a stupid risk and more like a necessity. Blending in here would be harder, if everyone was only here on their way to and from the installations on the moon. In my feed, ART said, *I told you so.*

The location for the meeting was a food service place

in the main mall area. It was in a large transparent bubble in the second level of the mall, overlooking the walkways and counter service stalls below. There were multiple open levels inside, with tables and chairs, and it was 40 percent full of humans and augmented humans. As I walked through, I picked up the occasional buzz of a drone, but no pings. There were food smells in the air, and the acrid scents of intoxicants. I didn't bother to try to analyze and identify them; I was too nervous and trying to focus on looking like an augmented human.

The humans I was to meet had sent an image so I could find them. There were three of them, all wearing variations on work clothes, no uniform logos. A quick search had shown entries for them in the transit ring's social feed. They had listed themselves as unaffiliated guest workers, but you could list yourself as anything, there was no identity check. Two were female, and one was tercera, which was a gender signifier used in the group of non-corporate political entities known as the Divarti Cluster.

(To initiate the meeting, I'd had to make an entry on the social feed, too. The system was extremely vulnerable to hacking, so I had backdated my entry to look like I had come in on an earlier passenger transport, listed my job as "security consultant," and my gender as indeterminate. Posing as its own captain, ART gave me a prior employment reference.)

I spotted them at a table near the bubble overlooking the mall. They were having a tense whispered conversation and body language said they were nervous. As I walked toward them, my quick scan showed no weapon signatures, just the small power sources of their personal feed interfaces. One had an implant, but it was just a low-level feed access tool.

I had practiced this part with ART on approach to the ring, recording myself so both of us could critique it. I told myself I could do this. I put on my best neutral expression, the one I used when the extra download activity had been detected and the deployment center's supervisor was blaming the human techs for it. I walked up to the table and said, "Hello."

All three of them flinched. "Uh, hello," the tercera said, recovering first.

I picked up the feed from the security camera so I could watch myself and make sure my facial expressions were under control. And it was easier to talk to the humans while watching them through the cameras. I was well aware it was a completely false sensation of distance from the situation, but I needed it. I said, "We arranged to meet. I'm Eden, the security consultant." Right, so, it was the name of one of the characters in *Sanctuary Moon*. You probably aren't surprised by that.

The tercera cleared ter throat. Te had purple hair and

red eyebrows, standing out against light brown skin. "I'm Rami, that's Tapan, and Maro." Te shifted nervously and tapped the empty chair.

ART, who was considerably faster than me at data retrieval, performed a quick search and informed me it was an invitation to sit down across several human cultural indices. It was giving me the etymology of the gesture as I sat down. You would think a SecUnit who had been shot to pieces multiple times, blown up, memory purged, and once partially dismantled by accident wouldn't be on the verge of panic under these circumstances. You'd be wrong.

Rami added, "Uh, I'm not sure where to start." Tapan nudged ter, apparently conveying moral support. Tapan had multicolored braids wrapped up around her head, and a blue jewel-toned interface clipped to her ear, and slightly darker skin than Rami. Maro had very dark skin, and silver-colored little puffs of hair, and was almost beautiful enough to be in the entertainment media. I'm terrible at estimating human ages because it's not one of the few things I care about. Also most of my experience is with the humans on the entertainment feed, and they aren't anything like the ones you see in reality. (One of the many reasons I'm not fond of reality.) But I thought all three might be young. Not children, but maybe not that far from adolescence.

They stared at me, and I realized I was going to have

to help. I said, cautiously, "You want to hire a security consultant?" This was what they had posted on the social feed, and from the number of similar requests, it was common for groups and individuals to hire private security before going to RaviHyral. I guess hiring human security guards is what you do when you can't afford real security.

Rami seemed relieved. "Yes, we need help."

Maro threw a look around and said, "We shouldn't talk here, maybe. Is there someplace else we could go?"

It had been stressful enough getting here, I didn't want to have to go anywhere else right now. I did a quick scan for drones, then initiated a glitch in the connection between the restaurant and transit ring security. I caught the cameras and showed ART what I wanted it to do. It took over and edited me out of the system's recording and cut the camera watching the table out of the system. I unglitched the connection to the ring's main security, which wouldn't notice the missing camera feed for the short time we would be here. I said, "It's all right. We're not being recorded."

They stared at me. Rami said, "But there's security— Did you do something?"

"I'm a security consultant," I repeated. My panic level was starting to drop, primarily because they were so obviously nervous. Humans are nervous of me because I'm a terrifying murderbot, and I'm nervous of them because they're humans. But I knew that humans could also be wary and nervous of each other in non-combat and non-adversarial situations, in reality and not just as part of a story. That was what seemed to be happening, but it let me pretend this was business as usual during one of the rare occasions when clients asked my advice about security.

Part of my job as a SecUnit was to give clients advice when they asked for it, as I was theoretically the one with all the information on security. Not that a lot of them had asked for it, or had listened to me. Not that I'm bitter about that, or anything.

Tapan looked impressed. "So you're spliced, right?" She patted the back of her neck, indicating where my data port was. "You got augments? You have extra access to the feed?"

"Spliced" was an informal term for an augmented human; I'd heard it on the entertainment feed. I said, "Yes." Then added, "Among other things."

Rami's red brows lifted in understanding. Maro looked impressed, and said, "I don't know if we can afford— Our credit account is— If we can get our data back, then—"

Rami took it up again. "Then we would have plenty to pay you."

ART, who was apparently very interested in the job scenario, started to search the public feeds for a pay scale for private security consultants. I reminded myself that I was pretending not to be a SecUnit, so me questioning them wouldn't seem out of the ordinary. I decided to start with the basic information. "Why do you want to hire me?"

Rami looked at the other two, got nods in response, and cleared ter throat. "We were working on Ravi-Hyral, for Tlacey Excavations, one of the smaller Umro contractors. We do mineral research and technology development." Te explained that they were a collective of technologists, seven of them plus dependents, who traveled from work contract to work contract. The others were waiting in a hotel suite, with Rami, Maro, and Tapan having been deputized to act for the group. It was a relief to hear that their mining experience was in tech and research; in the mining contracts I had had, the techs were usually in offices off the pit site or adjacent to it, and we didn't see them unless they got intoxicated and tried to kill each other, which admittedly was rare.

"Tlacey's terms were great," Tapan added, "but maybe too great, if you know what I mean."

ART did a quick search and returned the opinion that it was intended to be a figure of speech. I told it I knew that.

Rami continued, "We took the contract because it would give us time to work on our own stuff. We'd had this idea to develop a new detection system for strange synthetics. RaviHyral has a lot of identified deposits, so it's a great place for research." Strange synthetics were elements left behind by alien civilizations. Telling the difference between them and naturally occurring elements that were previously unidentified was a problem in mining. Like the remnants of alien occupation/civilization uncovered by GrayCris on my last contract, they were off limits for commercial development. That was all I'd ever needed to know, since every job I'd ever had involving alien material was just me standing around guarding the people who were working on it. (ART tried to explain it to me and I told it to save it for later, I needed to focus.)

Rami said, "We were making good progress, but then suddenly our group got terminated with no notice, and they took our data—"

Tapan waved her hands. "All our work! It wasn't anything to do with our contract—"

Maro finished, "Tlacey stole it, basically, and they deleted the most current version off our devices. We had copies of the older iterations, but we've lost all our recent work."

Rami added, "We filed a complaint with Umro, but it's taking forever to process it, and we don't know if it's ever going to come to anything."

I said, "This sounds like something you should go to a

solicitor about." It wasn't unusual. The company data mined, too, but it wasn't as clumsy or obvious as to try to delete the work from the original creators' devices. If it did that, then the creators wouldn't come back and enter into more security bond agreements, which would give the company access to whatever they were working on next.

"We thought about a solicitor," Rami said. "But we aren't in the union, so it would be expensive. But then yesterday Tlacey finally answered our petition, and said we could have the files back if we returned our signing bonus. We have to go down to RaviHyral to do that." Te sat back in ter chair. "That's why we wanted to hire you."

This was starting to make sense. "You don't trust Tlacey."

"We just want somebody on our side," Tapan clarified.

"No, we definitely don't trust Tlacey," Maro countered. "Not at all. We need security for when we get there, if things get . . . touchy. Tlacey herself is supposed to meet us, and she has an entourage of bodyguards, and there's no general security except what Umro has in the public areas and the port, and that's not much."

I didn't know exactly what she thought she meant by "touchy," but all the scenarios I could imagine in that situation weren't good ones.

The company offered SecUnits so the clients didn't

have to hire humans to guard each other. From what I had seen in the serials, me doing a half-assed version of my job was still better than a human trying to do it.

I was still watching us through the captured security camera even though I wasn't allowing it to record. I could see my expression was dubious, but in this case I think the situation warranted it. I said, "The meeting with Tlacey could be held through a secured comm channel." The company bonded those, too, for funds and data transfer.

Maro, whose expression was even more dubious than mine, said, "Yeah, but Tlacey wants to do it in person."

Rami admitted, "We know it doesn't sound like a good idea to go."

It was a great idea to go if you wanted to be murdered. I had hoped for an easier job, courier duty, or something similar. But this was protecting humans who were determined to do something dangerous, which was exactly the kind of job I was designed for. The job that I had kept doing more or less, often as less as possible, even after I had hacked my governor module. I was used to having something useful to do, taking care of something, even if it was only a contractually obligated group of humans who if I was lucky treated me like a tool and not a toy.

After PreservationAux, it had occurred to me how different it would be to do my job as an actual member of the group I was protecting. And that was the main reason I was here.

I phrased it as a question, because pretending you were asking for more information was the best way to try to get the humans to realize they were doing something stupid. "So do you think there's another reason Tlacey wants you to do this exchange in person, other than ... killing you?"

Tapan grimaced, as if that was something she had been aware of but trying not to think about. Maro tapped the table and pointed at me, which was vaguely alarming until ART identified it as a gesture of emphatic agreement. Rami took a sharp breath and said, "We think ... We weren't finished, our process was incomplete, but we were so enthusiastic about it ... We think they must have listened in using the security feeds and heard us talking, and thought we were much further along than we actually were. So I don't know if they can complete it. Maybe they realized it's not worth much without us to finish it."

"Maybe Tlacey wants us to work for her again," Tapan said hopefully.

Probably, before she murders you, I didn't say.

Maro snorted. "I would rather live in a box in a station mall than work for her again."

Once they had started to talk about it, it was hard for them to stop. The collective was completely divided on what to do, which was apparently painful for all of them since they were used to agreeing on everything. Tapan, who according to Maro was too naive for this existence, thought it was worth a try. Maro, who according to Tapan was a cynical impediment to both fun and progress, thought they were screwed and should just cut their losses. Rami was undecided, which was why te had been elected leader of the collective for the duration of this problem. Rami did not seem thrilled by the collective's confidence, but was gamely trying to proceed.

Finally, Rami finished up with, "So that's why we want to hire you. We thought it would be better to go in with someone who could protect us, keep her crew from messing with us, show her we have backup while we negotiate."

What they needed was a security company willing to bond them for the meeting and return trip, and send a SecUnit with them to guarantee their safety. But security companies like that are expensive, and wouldn't be interested in a job this small.

They all stared at me worriedly. In the security camera view, from that angle, it was obvious how small they were. They looked so soft, with all the fluffy multicolored hair. And nervous, but not of me. I said, "I accept your job."

Rami and Tapan looked relieved, and Maro, who clearly still didn't want to do this, looked resigned. She said, "How much do we pay you?" She glanced uncertainly at the others. "Can we afford you, I mean."

ART had a set of spreadsheets ready but I didn't want to scare them off with a figure that was too high. "How much were they paying you before you were terminated?"

Rami said, "It's two hundred CRs per cycle for each worker for the limited term of contract."

It didn't sound like this would take more than a cycle. "You can pay me that."

"One cycle's share of the contract?" Rami sat up straight. "Really?"

Ter reaction meant I'd asked for far too little, but it was too late to correct the mistake. I did need to give them a reason why I was willing to settle for a small amount, and I decided the partial truth was better. "I need to go to RaviHyral, and I need an employment contract to get there."

"Why?" Tapan asked, and Rami nudged her by way of admonishment. "I mean, I know we don't have a right to ask, but . . ."

Don't have a right to ask. That wasn't something that had ever applied to me, before PreservationAux. I told the truth again. "I need to do some research there for another client."

Like ART, they understood the idea of research, especially proprietary research, and they didn't ask any further questions. Rami told me they were scheduled to leave for RaviHyral during the next cycle, and said te would put in the request for the private employment voucher. I arranged to meet them in the mall near the access for the shuttle embarkation zone and then left. I released the security camera as soon as I was out of range.

I got back to ART and huddled in my favorite chair and we watched episodes for the next three hours while I calmed down. ART monitored the transit ring's alert feed in case someone had realized what I was, but there was nothing.

I told you so, ART said. Again.

I ignored it. I hadn't been detected, so now it was time to think about the rest of the plan. Which now involved keeping my new clients alive.

Chapter Five

I MET THEM AT the embarkation zone. I had the knapsack, which was part of my human disguise, but the only important thing I was carrying was the comm interface from ART. It would allow us to communicate once I was down on RaviHyral and let me continue to have access to ART's knowledge bases and unsolicited opinions. I was used to having a HubSystem and a SecSystem for backup and ART would be taking their place. (Without the part where those two systems were partly designed to rat me out to the company and trigger punishment through the governor module. ART's freedom to weigh in on everything I did was punishment enough.) I had inserted the comm interface in a built-in compartment under my ribs.

All three of my clients were waiting, each with a small bag or pack, since hopefully they would only be staying a couple cycles. I hung back until they finished saying goodbye to the other members of their collective. They all looked worried. The collective was listed in the social feed as a group marriage, and had five children of various sizes. Once the others had left and Rami, Maro, and Tapan were alone, I came forward.

"Tlacey bought us passage on a public shuttle," Rami told me. "That could be a good sign, right?"

"Sure," I said. It was a terrible sign.

The employment voucher got me through into the embarkation zone and there was no weapons scan. RaviHyral allowed private weapons and had a low security presence in public areas, which was one reason small groups of humans needed to hire private security consultants to go there. As we approached the shuttle's lock I sent to ART: *Can you scan the shuttle for energy anomalies without transit ring security detecting the activity?*

No, but I'll tell it I'm running scanning diagnostics and testing systems.

As we reached the lock, ART reported *No anomalies, 90 percent match to factory specs.*

That was normal, and meant if there was an explosive device, it was inert at the moment, buried somewhere inside the hull. Five other guest workers waited to board, and my scan read no energy signatures. They had stuffed packs and bags, indicating packing for a long-term stay. I let them board first, then slid in front of Maro and went through the lock, scanning as I went.

The shuttle was bot-driven and the only crew was one augmented human who seemed only there to check employment vouchers and shuttle passes. She looked at me and said, "There's only supposed to be three of you."

I didn't answer, being in the middle of wrestling the security system for control. It was an entirely separate system from the bot pilot, which was non-standard for the shuttles I was used to.

Tapan's chin jutted out. "This is our security consultant."

I had control of ShuttleSecSys, and deleted its attempt to alert the bot pilot and the crew member to the fact that it was compromised.

The crew member frowned, checked the voucher again, but didn't argue. We went on into the compartment where the other passengers were getting seated. They were stowing their possessions or talking quietly. I hadn't eliminated them as potential threats, but their behavior was lowering the probability at a steady rate.

I took a seat next to Rami as my clients got settled and pinged ART again. ART said, *I'm scanning for targeting anomalies and situation is currently clear.*

It meant it couldn't see anything on the moon aiming at us. If that was the plan, it wouldn't happen until we were underway. If somebody fired at the transit ring from the moon's surface, I was pretty sure that would be a huge deal and there would be legal ramifications, if not immediate violent retaliation by ring security. I told ART,

If they fire at us en route, it's not like we can do anything about it.

ART didn't answer, but I knew it well enough by now to know that meant something. I said, *You don't have a weapons system.* There hadn't been one on the schematics. At least the schematics that ART made available in its unsecured feed. *Do you?*

ART admitted, *I have a debris deflection system.*

There's only one way to deflect debris. I had never been on an armed ship but I knew they were subject to a whole different level of licensing and bond agreements. (If one of them accidentally shoots something it's not supposed to, somebody has to pay for the damage.) I said, *You have a weapons system.*

ART repeated, *For debris deflection.*

I was starting to wonder just what kind of university owned ART.

Rami was watching me worriedly. "Is everything okay?"

I nodded and tried to look neutral.

Tapan leaned past ter to ask, "Are you in the feed? I can't find you."

I told her, "I'm on a private channel with a friend in the ring who's monitoring the shuttle's departure. Just making sure everything's okay."

They nodded and sat back.

The shudder went through the deck that meant the shuttle had uncoupled from the ring and started to move. I cozied up to the bot pilot. It was a limited function model, not nearly as complex as even a standard transport driver bot. I had the ShuttleSecSys tell it I was authorized by ring security, and it pinged me cheerfully. The crew member was sitting in the cockpit with it, using her feed to catch up on admin tasks and read her social feed download, but there was no human pilot aboard.

I leaned back in my seat and relaxed a little. Media was tempting, and from the echoes I could pick up in the feed, that's what most of the humans were doing. But I wanted to keep monitoring the bot pilot. This may seem overcautious, but that's how I was built.

Then twenty-four minutes forty-seven seconds into the flight, as we were on approach, the bot pilot screamed and died as killware flooded its system. It was gone before ShuttleSecSys or I could react; I flung up a wall around us both and the killware bounced off. I saw it register task complete and then destroy itself.

Oh, shit. *ART!* I used ShuttleSecSys to grab the controls. We needed the course correction in seven point two seconds. The crew member, jolted out of her feed by the alarms, stared at the board in horror, then hit the emergency beacon. She couldn't fly a shuttle. I can fly hoppers and other upper atmosphere aircraft, but I had never been given the education module for shuttles or other space-going vehicles. I nudged ShuttleSecSys, hoping for help, and it set off all the cabin alarms. Yeah, that didn't help.

Let me in, ART said, as cool and calm as if we were discussing what show to watch next.

I had never given ART full access to my brain. I had let it alter my body, but not this. We had three seconds and counting. My clients, the other humans on the shuttle. I let it in.

It was like the sensation humans describe in books as having their heads shoved underwater. Then it was gone and ART was in the shuttle, using my connection with ShuttleSecSys to leap into the void left by the erased bot. ART flowed into the controls, made the course correction and adjusted our speed, then picked up the landing beacon and guided the shuttle into approach on the main RaviHyral port. The crew member had just managed to hail Port Authority, and was still hyperventilating. Port Authority had the ability to upload emergency landing routines, but the timing had been too tight. Nothing they could have done would have saved us.

Rami touched my arm and said, "Are you okay?"

I'd squeezed my eyes shut. "Yes," I told ter. Remembering that humans usually want more than that from other humans, I pointed up to indicate the alarms and added, "I've got sensitive hearing."

Rami nodded sympathetically. The others were worried, but there hadn't been an announcement and they could see our route in the feed from the port, which was still giving us an on-time arrival.

The crew member tried to explain to Port Authority that there had been a catastrophic failure, the pilot bot was gone, and she didn't know why the shuttle was following its normal route and not slamming into the surface of the moon. ShuttleSecSys tried to analyze ART and almost got itself deleted. I took over ShuttleSecSys, turned off the alarms, and deleted the entire trip out of its memory.

There were murmurs of relief from the passengers as the alarms stopped. I made a suggestion to ART, and it sent an error code to Port Authority, which assigned us a new priority and switched our landing site from the public dock to the emergency services dock. Since the killware had clearly been intended to destroy us en route, there might not be anybody waiting for us at our scheduled landing slot, but better safe than sorry.

The feed was giving us a visual of the port, which was inside a cavern, carved out of the side of a mountain, surrounded by the towers of a debris deflection grid. (An actual debris deflection system, as opposed to ART's concealed rail gun or whatever it had.) The lights of multiple levels of the port installation gleamed in the darkness, and smaller shuttles whizzed out of our way as we curved down toward the Port Authority's beacon.

Maro was watching me with narrowed eyes. When the notice of changed landing site came through the feed, she leaned forward and said, "You know what happened?"

Fortunately I remembered that nobody expected me to be compelled to answer all questions immediately. One of the benefits to being an augmented human security consultant rather than a construct SecUnit. I said, "We'll talk about it when we're off the shuttle," and they all seemed satisfied.

ART landed us in the Port Authority's slot. We left the shuttle crew member trying to explain to the emergency techs what had happened as they connected their diagnostic equipment. ART was already gone, deleting any evidence of its presence, and the ShuttleSecSys was confused, but at least still intact, unlike the poor pilot bot.

Emergency services personnel and bots milled around the small embarkation zone. I managed to herd my clients through and out onto the clear enclosed walkway to the main port before anyone thought to try to stop them. I had already downloaded a map from the public feed and was testing the robustness of the security system. The walkway had a view of the cavern, with the multiple levels of landing slots and a few shuttles coming and going. At the far end were the big haulers for the mining installations.

Security seemed to be intermittent and based on the level of paranoia of whatever contractor operated in the territory you were passing through. That could be both an advantage and an interesting challenge. The transit ring's public info feed had warned that a lot of humans apparently carried weapons here, and there were no screening scans.

We came out into a central hub, which had a high clear dome allowing a view of the cavern arching overhead, with lights trained on it to show off the colorful mineral veins. I scanned to make sure nothing was recording us and stopped Rami. Te and the others looked up at me and I said, "The person you're going to meet with just tried to kill you."

Rami blinked, Maro went wide-eyed, and Tapan drew breath to argue. I said, "The shuttle was infected with killware. It destroyed the bot pilot. I was in contact with a friend who was able to use my augmented feed to download a new pilot module. That's the only reason we didn't crash."

A module could have put the shuttle into a safe orbit, but wouldn't have been sophisticated enough to manage the tricky, flawless landing. I was hoping they wouldn't realize that.

Tapan closed her mouth. Shocked, Maro said, "But the other passengers. The crew person. They would have killed everybody?"

I said, "If you were the only casualties, the motive would have been obvious."

I could see it was starting to sink in. I said, "You should return to the transit ring immediately." I checked the public feed for the schedule. There was a public shuttle leaving in eleven minutes. Tlacey wouldn't have time to trace my clients and infect it if they moved fast.

Tapan and Maro looked at Rami. Te hesitated, then set ter jaw and said, "I'll stay. You two go."

"No," Maro said instantly, "we're not leaving you." Tapan added, "We're in this together."

Rami's face almost crumpled, their support weakening ter when the prospect of death hadn't. Te controlled terself and nodded tightly. Te looked at me and said, "We'll stay."

I didn't react visibly, because I'm used to clients making bad decisions, and I was getting a lot of practice at controlling my expression. "You can't keep this meeting. They lost track of you when the shuttle didn't dock at its scheduled slot. You have to keep that advantage."

"But we have to have the meeting," Tapan protested. "We can't get our work back otherwise."

Yes, I often want to shake my clients. No, I never do. "Tlacey has no intention of giving you back your work. She lured you here to kill you."

"Yes, but—" Tapan began.

"Tapan, just hush and listen," Maro interrupted, clearly exasperated.

Rami looked stubborn, but asked, "Then what should we do?"

Technically, this didn't have to be my problem. I was here now and didn't need them anymore. I could lose them in the crowd and leave them to deal with their murderous ex-employer all on their own.

But they were clients. Even after I'd hacked my governor module, I'd found it impossible to abandon clients I hadn't chosen. I'd made an agreement with these clients as a free agent. I couldn't leave. I kept my sigh internal. "You can't meet Tlacey at her compound. You'll pick the spot."

It wasn't ideal, but it would have to do.

My clients picked a food service place in the center of the port. It was on a raised platform, the tables and chairs arranged in groups, with displays floating above advertising various port and contractor services and information about the different mining installations. The displays also functioned as camera and recording chaff, so the place was a popular spot for business meetings.

Rami, Tapan, and Maro had picked a table and were nervously fiddling with the drinks they had ordered from one of the bots drifting around. They had put in a comm call to Tlacey, and were waiting for a representative to arrive.

The security system in this public area was more sophisticated than ShuttleSecSys but not by much. I had gotten in far enough to monitor emergency traffic and get views from the cameras focused on our immediate area. I felt pretty confident. I was standing three meters from the table, pretending to look at the ad displays and examining the map of the installations I had found in the public feed. There were plenty of abandoned dig sites marked, as well as tube accesses that went off into apparently nowhere. Ganaka Pit had to be one of them.

ART said in my ear, *There must be an accessible information archive. Ganaka Pit's existence would not be deleted from it. The absence would be too obvious to researchers.*

That depended on the research. Someone working on strange synthetics would obviously care about where they were found, but not necessarily about what company had dug them up, or why that company wasn't around anymore. But whoever had removed Ganaka Pit from the map would have been trying to obscure its existence from casual journalists, not erase it entirely from the memory of the population.

ART's data had been correct; there were other SecUnits on this moon. The map showed logos from five bond companies that offered SecUnits, including my company, at seven of the most remote installations where exploration for mineral veins was still ongoing. They would be there to defend the claim from theft and to keep the miners and other employees from injuring each other as part of the bond guarantee. No SecUnits would travel through the port except as inert cargo in transport boxes or repair cubicles, so that was one less thing to worry about. My altered configuration might fool humans and augmented humans, but not other SecUnits.

If they saw me, they would alert their SecSystems. They wouldn't have a choice. And they wouldn't want one. If anybody knows how dangerous rogue SecUnits are, it's other SecUnits.

That was when I felt the ping.

I told myself I'd mistaken it for something else. Then it happened again. That's a big uh-oh.

Something was looking for SecUnits. Not just bots, specifically SecUnits, and it was close. It hadn't pinged me directly, though if I'd had a working governor module, I would have been compelled to answer.

Three humans approached the table my clients were sitting at. Rami whispered into ter feed, "That's Tlacey. I didn't expect her to come herself." Two of the humans were large and male and one of them lengthened his stride to reach the table. Maro had seen him and from the look on her face I knew this was not going to be a greeting. Scan showed he was armed.

I moved between him and the table. I put a hand up at his chest height and said, "Stop."

On most contracts this was as far as I was allowed to go with a human until they made physical contact. But you'd be surprised how often this works, if you do it right. Though that was when I was wearing my armor with the helmet opaqued. Standing here in normal human clothes with my human face showing made it a whole different thing. But it wasn't like he could hurt me by hitting me and he hadn't drawn his weapon yet.

I could have torn through him like tissue paper.

He didn't know that, but he must have been able to tell from my face that I wasn't afraid of him. I checked the security camera to see what I looked like, and decided I looked bored. That wasn't unusual, because I almost always looked bored while I was doing my job, it was just impossible to tell when I was in my armor.

He visibly regrouped and said, "Who the fuck are you?"

My clients had shoved their chairs back and were on their feet. Rami said, "This is our security consultant."

He stepped back, and glanced uncertainly at the other two, the second male human bodyguard and Tlacey, who was an augmented human female.

I dropped my arm but didn't move. I had clear shots at all three of them, but that was a worst-case scenario. For me, at least. Humans can miss a lot of little clues, but me being able to fire energy weapons from my arms would be something of a red flag. I diverted just enough attention to scan the security camera feeds for whatever it was that had pinged me.

I caught an image on a camera across the public area, near one of the entrance tunnels. The figure standing near the edge of the seating area didn't match what I was expecting to see and I had to review it again before I understood. It wasn't wearing armor and its physical configuration didn't match SecUnit standard. It had a lot of hair, silver with blue and purple on the ends, pulled back and braided like Tapan's but in a much more complicated pattern. Its facial features were different from mine, but all Units' features are different, assigned randomly based on the human cloned material that's used to make our organic parts. Its arms were bare, and there was no metal showing and no gun ports. This was not a SecUnit.

I was looking at a sexbot.

That is not the official designation, ART said.

The official designation is ComfortUnit but everybody knows what that means.

Sexbots aren't allowed to walk around in human areas without orders, any more than murderbots. Someone must have sent it here.

ART poked me hard enough to make me twitch. I snapped out of it and ran my recording back a little to catch up on what was happening.

Tlacey had stepped forward. "And just why do you need a security consultant?"

Rami took a breath. I hit ter feed, secured a private connection between ter, Tapan, and Maro, and told ter, *Don't answer that. Don't mention the attempt on the shuttle. Just stick to business.* It was an impulse. Tlacey had come here expecting an angry confrontation; that was why she had brought armed bodyguards. We had an advantage now; we weren't dead, and they were off balance and we wanted to keep them that way.

Rami let the breath out, tapped my feed in acknowledgment, then said, "We're here to talk about our files."

Maro, who had realized what I was trying to do, told Rami, *Keep going, don't even let them sit down.*

Sounding more confident, Rami continued, "Deleting our personal work was not part of our employment contract. But we'll agree to your proposal that we return our signing bonus in exchange for our files."

On the security cameras, I watched the sexbot turn and leave the public area via the tunnel directly behind it.

Tlacey said, "The entire bonus?" She clearly hadn't expected them to agree.

Maro leaned forward. "We opened an account with Umro to hold the funds. We can transfer it to you as soon as you give us the files."

Tlacey's jaw moved as she spoke in her private feed. The two bodyguards eased back. Tlacey stepped over and took a chair at my clients' table. After a moment, Rami sat down, and Tapan and Maro followed suit.

I kept part of my attention on the negotiation, and went back to the public feed. I started pulling historical data, looking for any irregular activity around the time of my contract here.

While my clients were talking, and while I sorted through the data with ART peering over my shoulder again, I was watching the security cameras. I noted two more potential threats enter the area. Both were augmented humans. I had noted three potential threats already sitting at adjacent tables. (All three exhibited a curious lack of attention toward the confrontation occurring near the center of the seating area. The other humans and augmented humans in the immediate area had watched it with open or surreptitious curiosity.)

ART poked me. *I see it,* I told it. The search had turned up a series of notices posted around the right timeframe. They were warnings that changes in shipments of raw materials and supplies to outlying installations would cause diversions in the passenger tube routes. (The tube was a small-scale transit system that took passengers around the port and service centers and had private lines going out to the closer mining installations.) Later notices mentioned a new route that had been constructed to compensate for the diversion.

That was it. Reading between the lines, you could see that the service contractors had had to build a new tube route to bypass the tunnels that had led to a mining installation that had abruptly closed. That had to be the site of Ganaka Pit.

Other pit closures had been accompanied by local interest articles and excessive social feed interest in bankruptcy filings and the effect on the associated service companies. There was nothing like that about this closure. Someone had paid to have those postings deleted from the public feed.

The conversation was concluding. Tlacey stood up,

nodded to my clients, and walked away from the table. Rami's expression was a grimace of doubt. Maro looked grim and Tapan somewhere between confused and angry.

I closed the search and stepped over to the table. Watching Tlacey and her bodyguards leave, Rami said, "It was a bad idea to come here."

Tapan protested, "She said tomorrow..."

Maro shook her head. "It's more lies. She isn't going to give us the files. She could have done it here, if she was going to do it. She could have done it over the comm while we were on the transit ring." She looked up at me. "I wasn't sure I believed you about the shuttle, but now..."

I was keeping track of my potential threat list on the security cameras. "We need to go," I told them. "We'll talk about this somewhere else."

As we left, one potential threat got up to follow us. I tapped ART to keep an eye on the others, just in case they weren't innocent bystanders so deep in their feeds they really hadn't noticed anything.

I had marked a few possible routes on the station map, and my favorite one was through a pedestrian tunnel that curved out away from the main living areas. There were various accesses along it leading to different tube stations, but it was not a popular route. I tapped Rami's feed and told ter to take it toward the interchange where the largest hotel was. Listening in, Maro whispered, "We can't afford that one."

You won't be staying there, I told them on the feed. The brochure on the public feed promised a high security lobby area and a fast tube access to the public shuttle slots.

We reached the tunnel and started down it. It was close to ten meters wide and four meters high, well-lit enough for walking down the center, but the sides were shadowy with darkened branching tunnels. There were security cameras, but the system monitoring them was not sophisticated. The company would have shit itself over the possible danger to bonded clients and the missed opportunity to data mine conversations.

There were other humans in the tunnel. Some miners in coveralls and jackets with logos from the various installations, but most were in civilian work clothes, either techs or workers for the support companies. They moved quickly and stayed in groups.

After eight minutes of walking, most of the other humans in the tunnel had turned off to one of the tube access points. I sent through the feed, *Just keep walking, don't stop. I'll meet you in the lobby.* I dropped back into one of the darker branching tunnels. My clients kept moving and didn't look back at me, though I could tell Tapan wanted to.

On the cameras I watched Potential Threat/New Target

make his way up the tunnel, walking quickly. He was joined by two new humans, now designated Target Two and Target Three. They passed me and I came out of the tube access and followed at a distance. I scanned them for energy weapons and found no readings. All three Targets wore jackets and pants with deep side pockets. I marked seven locations where knives or extendable batons could be carried.

When they caught sight of my clients, the Targets slowed down but continued to reduce the distance between them. I knew they were probably reporting to someone on their feed, asking for instructions. Whoever it was didn't have control of the security cameras, at least not yet.

I followed, watching the targets through my eyes, through the security cameras, watching myself to make sure I wasn't drawing attention, that no one was following me. ART kept quiet, though I could tell it was interested in watching me work.

Then the last group of miners between me and the Targets turned into a tube access. We were in a bend of the tunnel and there was no one between my clients and the next bend some fifty meters ahead, and the security cameras showed me the tunnel was empty behind me. I needed to get this over with. I turned into the tube access behind the miners.

I stopped at the top of the tube access while the miners boarded the capsule. The door hissed as it closed and the capsule moved away. On security camera view, Target Two's jaw moved, indicating that he was speaking subvocally in his feed. Then the camera's feed cut off.

I turned the corner back into the tunnel and started to run.

It was a calculated risk, as I couldn't move at top speed without revealing I wasn't human. But I managed to arrive just as Target One reached Rami and grabbed the sleeve of ter jacket. I broke his arm and slammed an elbow into his chin, then swung him into Target Two, who had turned toward me with the knife he had been approaching Maro with. Target Two accidentally (I'm guessing here; maybe they just didn't care for each other) stabbed Target One. Target Two staggered sideways and I dropped Target One, and broke Target Two's kneecap. Target Three had had time to lift his baton and now hit me across the left side of my head and shoulder which, granted, annoyed me a little, but I've had hauler bots hit me harder than that by accident. I blocked the second blow with my left arm, snapped his collarbone with one punch, and smashed his hip with another.

He was lucky I wasn't a lot annoyed.

All three Targets were on the floor, and Two was the

only one who was still conscious, though he was curled up and whimpering. I turned to my clients.

Rami had a hand over ter mouth, Maro was frozen in place, staring, and Tapan had thrown her hands up in the air. I said in the feed, *Go to the hotel, wait for me in the lobby. Don't run, walk.*

Maro came out of shock first. She nodded hard, caught Rami's arm, and poked Tapan's shoulder. Rami turned to go, but Tapan said, "Security?"

I knew what she was asking. "They told somebody to cut the cameras. That's why you need to leave now." The public feed up on the transit ring had said there was no overall security, but the security companies for the different service installations and contractors were supposed to take responsibility for the public areas nearest their territory. This spot had obviously been carefully calculated to be out of range of any immediate assistance by whoever had helped the Targets by cutting the camera feed. I wasn't expecting an immediate response, but we did need to move relatively quickly.

Rami whispered, "Come on," and they started away, walking fast but not running.

I turned to the Target that was still conscious and pressed down on the artery in his neck until he passed out.

I started away, walking at a normal pace. I was deep enough into the camera system to delete the temporary storage on the cameras ahead of and behind the deactivated camera. That would help obscure the issue for anybody trying to figure out what had happened. But Tlacey had seen me, and she would know. I was just hoping the kids listened to me this time.

I reached the interchange where various access tunnels and tube stations met, with a scatter of pop-up stands selling packaged food, feed interfaces, toiletries, and other things humans liked. It wasn't crowded but there was a steady flow of foot traffic. The hotel entrance was on the far side.

The lobby was built on various platforms overlooking a holo sculpture of an open chasm filled with a giant crystalline structure growing out of the walls. From the notations in the feed, it was supposed to be educational, but I had serious doubts about whether the mines on Ravi-Hyral looked like that. Especially after the mining bots got to them.

My clients were on the same platform as the check-in area, near the railing around the sculpture's artificial chasm, sitting on a round backless couch thing that looked more like a decorative object than furniture.

I sat on my heels in front of them.

Rami said, "They were going to kill us."

"Again," I said.

Rami bit ter lip. "I believed you about the shuttle. I believed you . . ."

"But now you've seen it," I said. I knew what te meant. There was a huge difference between knowing something happened and seeing the reality of it. Even for SecUnits.

Maro rubbed her eyes. "Yeah, we were idiots. Tlacey was never going to let us give her the bonus for our files."

"No, she wasn't," I agreed.

Rami nudged her. "You were right."

Maro looked more depressed. "I didn't want to be."

Tapan said miserably, "We're wrecked."

Rami put an arm around her. "We're alive." Te looked at me. "What do we do now?"

I said, "Let me get you out of here."

Chapter Six

I TOOK THEM TO the public shuttle slots first, then past that section to the private docks. Checking the schedules, ART had already scanned a likely shuttle. It was privately owned but the frequency of its trips to and from the transit ring suggested an entrepreneur who was offering private rides for hard currency.

This proved to be accurate, and it would allow Rami, Maro, and Tapan to leave without their employment vouchers being scanned. It would probably have been safe at this point to put them on a public shuttle, as long as there was no advance notice of which one they were taking. Killware couldn't travel over the feed to infect a shuttle; there were too many protections in place. Whoever had planned to kill us on arrival had had to deliver the killware directly, through a data port actually inside the shuttle's cockpit.

But I'm programmed to be paranoid. This private shuttle had the benefit not only of anonymity, but of an augmented human pilot who would be in place in case something interfered with the bot pilot. Plus ART, who was already cozying up to said bot pilot and would be keeping an eye on the shuttle during the brief trip. (ART's idea of "cozying" being somewhat overbearing, I had already had to intervene once to assure the bot pilot that the big mean transport had promised not to hurt it.)

"You're not going with us?" Rami asked, standing in the small embarkation area. The private docks were dingy and small compared to the Port Authority's docks, with stains on the metal partitions and some of the lights up in the rocky ceiling broken or dim. Humans and a few bots were moving along the walkway above us, and I kept an eye on both approaches through the security cameras. The shuttle was already loaded into its slot and its hatch was open, with a small augmented human standing on the ramp to take the money. Six other passengers had already boarded and it was taking a large portion of my self-control not to just scoop up my clients and carry them onboard.

I said, "I still need to do some research here. I'll go back to the transit ring when I'm finished."

"How do we pay you?" Maro asked. "I mean, can we still afford you after . . . everything?" *After they tried to kill us,* she added in our joint feed connection.

"I'll check my social feed profile on the ring," I said, and felt pretty good that I had even remembered it existed. "Send a note to me there, and I'll find you when I get back."

"It's just, I know we're—" Tapan glanced around. Her expression was tense and unhappy, her body language bordering on desperate. "We can't stay here, but I can't give up, either. Our work—"

I said, "Sometimes people do things to you that you can't do anything about. You just have to survive it and go on."

They all stopped talking and stared at me. It made me nervous and I immediately switched my view to the nearest security camera so I could watch us from the side. I had said it with more emphasis than I intended, but it was just the way things were. I wasn't sure why it had such an impact on them. Maybe I sounded like I knew what I was talking about. Maybe it was the two murder attempts.

Then Maro nodded, her mouth set in a grim line. She and Rami looked at each other and Rami nodded sadly. Maro said, "We need to get back to the others, figure out what to do next. Look for the next assignment."

Rami added, "We'll start over. We did it once, we can do it again."

Tapan looked like she wanted to protest, but was too depressed to argue.

They wanted to say goodbye a lot and thank me, and I herded them up to the ramp while they were doing it, and watched Rami pay for their passage with a currency card that the crew person pressed to an interface. Then they were aboard.

The hatch closed and the shuttle's feed signaled postboarding mode, waiting for its clearance to leave. I went back down the access, heading for the walkway. I needed to get the tube over to the area where the tunnel diversion had occurred and start searching for Ganaka Pit. It was a relief to have my clients headed back to safety. But it felt odd to be on my own again, working for no one except myself.

I went to the tube access and boarded the next capsule to stop. Each capsule had seating for twenty people, plus an overhead rack to hold on to. The gravity was adjusted inside the cab to compensate for the motion. I took a seat with the seven humans already aboard. ART said, *The shuttle has launched. I'll monitor your feed, but much of my attention will be on it.*

I sent an acknowledgment. I was trying to isolate why I felt so uneasy. Trapped in a small enclosed space with humans, check. Missing my drones, check. My Giant Asshole Research Transport too busy to complain at, check. Needed to actually focus on what I was doing so couldn't watch media, check. But that wasn't what it was. I hadn't done a good job for my clients. I had had the opportunity, and had failed. As a SecUnit, I had the responsibility for my clients' safety but no authority to do anything other than make suggestions, and try to use the company regulations inbuilt in a SecSystem to override the humans' suicidal stupidity and homicidal impulses. This time I had responsibility and authority, and had still failed.

I told myself they were alive, I just hadn't gotten their property back, which had actually not been part of the job they hired me for. It didn't help.

I got off the tube on the far end of its circuit. This was a warren of tunnels that according to the map led off to various private tube accesses for the distant mining pits. Only a few humans got off the tube here, all heading immediately down the tunnel for the nearest tube interchange. I went the other direction.

I spent the next hour hacking cameras and security barriers, slipping in and out of half-completed tunnels, many with warning markers for air quality. Finally I located one that showed evidence of past use as a mining access. It was big enough for the largest hauler bots, and the cameras and lights were down. As I went along it, climbing over rock and metal debris, I felt the public feed drop out.

I stopped and checked ART's comm, but it was only picking up static. I didn't think it was any deliberate attempt to block my connection to the rest of the installation; I'd experienced that type of outage before and this felt different. I think this tunnel was so deep below the surface that the comm and the feed needed powered relays to get out, and those weren't functioning anymore. Something ahead still had power, because my feed was picking up intermittent signals, all automated warnings. I kept going.

I had to open another security barrier, but past it found a cargo tube access and managed to push the sliding door open. A small passenger tube was still there. It hadn't been used in a long time, long enough for the water and scattered trash on the carpet to combine and grow something squishy. I made my way up to the front compartment where the manual emergency controls were. There was still power in the batteries, though not much. It had been left here, forgotten, slowly dying in the darkness as the hours ticked away.

Not that I was feeling morbid, or anything.

I checked to make sure there was no active security attached to it, then got it started. It groaned into life, lifted off the ground, and started down the tunnel into darkness, following its last programmed route. I sat down on the bench to wait.

Finally the tube's scan picked up a blockage ahead and threw an alarm code. I had five episodes of different drama series, two comedies, a book about the history of the exploration of alien remnants in the Corporation Rim, and a multi-part art competition from Belal Tertiary Eleven queued and paused, but I was actually watching episode 206 of *Sanctuary Moon*, which I'd already seen twenty-seven times. Yes, I was a little nervous. When the tube started to slow, I sat up.

The lights shone on a line of metal barricades. Glowing markers had been sprayed on the material, sending out bursts of warning into my feed. Radiation hazard, falling rock hazard, toxic biological hazard. I got the emergency lock to unseal for me and jumped down to the gritty ground. I was scanning for energy signatures and I adjusted my eyesight to be able to see past the bright marker paint. There was a gap three meters along, a darker patch against the metal. It was small but I didn't have to pop any joints to wriggle through.

I walked down the tunnel to the platform that had been part of the passenger tube access. Farther down there was a set of ten-meter-high doors, big enough for vehicles and the largest hauler bots to maneuver through and for the loads of raw mineral to come out. The passenger access had a cargo unloading rack still extended, and I used it to swing up to the high platform. Everything was covered with a layer of damp dust, which showed no recent tracks. The sealed crates of a supply delivery, with the logos of various contractors stamped on the boxes, still stood stacked on the platform. A broken breather mask lay beside it. My human parts were experiencing a cold prickling that wasn't comfortable. This place was creepy. I reminded myself that the terrible thing that had most likely happened here was me.

Somehow that didn't help.

There wasn't enough power to move the doors, but the manual release for the passenger access lock still worked. There was no powered light in the corridor either, but the walls were streaked with light-emitting markers, meant to guide everyone out in the event of a catastrophic failure. Some had already failed with age, others were fading. The lack of any feed activity except from the warning paint was vaguely disturbing; I kept thinking of the DeltFall habitat and I was glad I had had ART make the adjustment to my data port.

I followed the corridor into the installation's central hub. It was a large domed area, dark except for the fading markers on the ground. There were no human remains, of course, but debris was scattered around, tools, broken slivers of plastic, a chunk of hauler bot arm. Openings to corridors, like dark caves, branched off in all directions. I had no sense of having been here before, no sense of familiarity. I identified the passages that led toward the mine pit, then the corridors that went toward the quarters and offices. Branching off from that was the equipment storage.

The emergency power failure releases for the sealed doors had unlocked everything, but whoever had cleaned up afterward had left them shut, and I had to shove each one open. Past the maintenance stations for the hauler bots, I found the security ready room. I stepped in and froze. In the dimness, among the empty weapon storage boxes and the missing floor panels where the recycler had stood, there were familiar shapes. The cubicles were still here.

There were ten of them lined up against the far wall, big smooth white boxes, the dim marker light gleaming off the scuffed surfaces. I didn't know why my performance reliability was dropping, why it was so hard to move. Then I realized it was because I thought the others were still in there.

It was a completely irrational thought that would have confirmed ART's bad opinion of the mental abilities of constructs. They wouldn't leave SecUnits here. We were too expensive, too dangerous to abandon. If I wasn't locked inside one of these cubicles, the organic part of my brain dreaming, the rest helpless and inert, then the others weren't here.

It was still hard to make myself cross the room and open the first door.

The plastic bed inside was empty, the power long cut off. I opened each one, but it was the same.

I stepped back from the last one. I wanted to bury my face in my hands, sink down to the floor, and slip into my media, but I didn't. After twelve long seconds, the intense feeling subsided.

I don't even know why I'd come in here. I needed to look for data storage, records left behind. I checked the weapons lockers to make sure there was nothing handy, like a package of drones, but they were empty. A firefight had left burn scars on the wall and there was a small crater impact from an explosive projectile next to one of the cubicles. Then I went back toward the offices.

I found the installation control center. Broken display surfaces were everywhere, chairs overturned, interfaces shattered on the floor, and a plastic cup still sat on a console, undisturbed, waiting for someone to pick it up again. Humans can't work completely in the feed with multiple inputs the way I can, and bots like ART can. Some augmented humans have implanted interfaces that allow it, but not all humans want lots of things inserted into their brains, go figure. So they need these surfaces to project displays for group work. And the external data storage should be tied in here somewhere.

I picked a station, set a chair upright, and got out the small toolkit I had borrowed from ART's crew storage and brought along in the large side pocket of my pants. (Armor doesn't have pockets, so score one for ordinary human clothing.) I needed a power source to get the station operable again, but fortunately I had me.

I used the tools to open a port on the energy weapon in my right forearm. Doing it one-handed was tricky, but I've had to do worse. I used a patch cord to connect me to the console's emergency power access and then the station hummed as it powered up. I couldn't open the feed to control it directly, but I reached into the glittering projection and fished out the access for the Security Systems recorded storage. It had been wiped, but I'd been expecting that.

I started to check all the other storage, just in case it hadn't been the company techs who had wiped SecSystem. The company wants everything recorded, work done in the feed, conversations, everything, so they can data mine it. A lot of that information is useless and gets deleted, but SecSystem has to hold on to it until the data mining bots can go over it, and so SecSystem often steals unused temporary storage space from other systems.

And there they were, files tucked into the MedSystem's storage space for non-standard procedure downloads. (Presumably if MedSystem suddenly needed to download an emergency procedure for a patient, SecSystem would have whisked the files out and put them somewhere else, but sometimes it couldn't act in time and chunks of recorded data would be lost. If you're a SecUnit and you like your clients and want to keep something they've said or done (or that you've said or done) away from the company, this is one of the many ways you can make files accidentally disappear.)

SecSystem must have shifted files over right before the power failure. There was a lot of material and I skipped past random conversations and mining operations data to the end, then scrolled back a little. In the feed, two human techs had discussed an anomaly, some code that didn't seem to be associated with any system, that had been uploaded on-site. They were trying to figure out where it had come from, and speculating, with a lot of profanity, that the installation had been bombed with malware. One tech said she was going to notify the supervisor, that they needed to sequester SecSystem, and the conversation ended there, in mid-word.

That was . . . not what I was expecting. I'd assumed a malfunction of my governor module had caused the massacre the company euphemistically referred to as an "incident." But had I really taken out nine other SecUnits, plus all the bots and any armed humans who might have tried to stop me? I didn't like my chances. If the other SecUnits had experienced the same malfunction, it had to come from an outside source.

I saved the conversation to my own storage, checked the other systems for stray files but found nothing, and unhooked myself from the console.

The security ready room had been stripped to the bone. But there were other places I could check. I pushed away from the console.

As I went through the other door, I noticed the impact points in the wall opposite, the stains on the floor. Someone—something capable of taking a high degree of injury had made a last stand here, trying to defend the control center. Maybe not all the SecUnits had been affected.

In the corridor near the living quarters, I found the other ready room, the one for the ComfortUnits.

Inside were four shapes that were clearly cubicles, but smaller. Their doors stood open, the plastic beds inside empty. In the corner there was space for a recycler, but no weapons lockers, and the storage cabinets were all different.

I stood in the center of the room. The cubicles for the murderbots had been closed, not in use. Which meant none of the SecUnits had been damaged and all had been either out on patrol, on guard, or in the ready room, probably standing around pretending not to stare at each other. But the cubicles for the sexbots were open, which meant they had been inside when the emergency occurred and the power shut off. If the power is off, you can manually open a cubicle from the inside, but it won't shut again.

It meant they had deployed during the "incident."

I used the energy weapon in my arm again to power the first cubicle's emergency data storage. I didn't have anywhere near the energy needed to get the whole thing powered up, but the data storage box is for holding error and shutdown information if something goes wrong during a repair. (There are a lot of other things you can do with it if you've hacked your governor module, like use it to temporarily store your media so the human techs won't find it.) SecSystem might have used it before its catastrophic failure.

It had been used. But by the ComfortUnits, to download their data during the incident.

It was patchy and hard to put together, until I realized the ComfortUnits had been communicating with each other.

I stood there for five hours and twenty-three minutes, putting the data fragments together.

There had been a code download from another mining installation for the ComfortUnits, supposedly a patch purchased from a third party ComfortUnit supplier. The ComfortUnits had all flagged it as non-standard and needing review by SecSystem and the human systems analyst, but the techs who had downloaded it ordered them to apply it. It turned out to be well-disguised malware. It hadn't affected the ComfortUnits, but had used their feeds to jump to SecSystem and infect it. SecSystem had infected the SecUnits, bots, and drones, and everything capable of independent motion in the installation had lost its mind.

In between the running and shooting and the humans screaming in the background, the ComfortUnits had managed to analyze the malware and discover it was supposed to jump from them to the hauler bots and shut them down. This would disrupt operations so the other mining installation could get their shipment to the cargo transport first. This had been a sabotage attempt, not a mass murder. But a mass murder was what was happening.

The humans had managed to get an alert out to the port, but it was clear help would not arrive in time. The ComfortUnits noted that the SecUnits were not acting in concert, and were also attacking each other, while the bots randomly smashed into anything that moved. The ComfortUnits had decided that taking SecSystem back to factory default via its manual interface was their best option.

ComfortUnits are more physically powerful than a human, but not a SecUnit or bot. They had no inbuilt weapons, and while they could pick up a projectile or energy weapon and use it, they had no education modules on how the weapons worked. They could pick one up, try to aim it, pull the trigger, and hope the safety wasn't engaged.

One by one the file downloads had stopped. One had signaled that it would try to decoy SecUnit attention away from the others, and three acknowledged. One had heard screams from the control center and diverted there to try to save the humans trapped inside, and two acknowledged. One had stayed at the entrance to a corridor to try to buy time to reach SecSystem, and one acknowledged. One reported reaching SecSystem, then nothing.

I caught a low power warning from my own system and realized how long I had been here. I unhooked myself from the cubicle and left the room. I bumped into the edge of the doorway and the wall.

There must have been some off-the-books arrangement, maybe the installation who supplied the malware paid for the damages and the bonds, which might have been such a large amount that the installation had then failed and ceased operation. Maybe the company thought that was punishment enough.

I made my way back to the tube, climbed inside, and

started a recharge cycle. Once I had enough capacity, I went back to episode 206 of *Sanctuary Moon*.

The tube ran out of power and died short of the access, but fortunately I was back up to 97 percent capacity by that time. I got out and ran the rest of the way. Running isn't tiring for me the way it is for a human, but I reached the sealed access fifty-eight minutes later than I would have on the tube.

It had been a long, shitty cycle, and I was ready for it to be over with. I wanted to get off this mine only slightly less than I had probably wanted to get off it the first time I was here.

I had gotten back through the security barrier and was walking up the tunnel when I came within range of the feed again. I tapped ART to let it know I was back.

It said, *We have a problem.*

Chapter Seven

I LOCATED THE PROBLEM in the lobby of the main hotel.

Tapan was on one of the upper platforms, seated on a round cushioned bench, her pack at her feet, partially screened by another holographic sculpture of a giant crystal formation. She looked up at me and said, "Oh, hi. I didn't know if the others would be able to reach you."

Without me present in the shuttle, ART hadn't had any visual access to the passenger compartment. (As a private vehicle that was only being used as a public transport in a sketchy if not openly illegal way, it had no onboard security system or cameras.) ART hadn't known Tapan wasn't onboard until the shuttle reached the transit ring. Taking its responsibility seriously, it had sent a drone over to the embarkation area to watch my clients disembark and had seen an obviously distraught and angry Rami and Maro, but no Tapan. Then it had checked Eden's profile on the social media feed and found the message from Rami. (Tapan had told them she was sick and was going to the shuttle's restroom compartment. They hadn't realized what had happened until the shuttle had cleared the port.)

I said, "They left me a message." I had intended to just stand there and stare at her, which is what SecUnits do to clients who have just performed an act of stupidity so profound it approaches suicide which they ordered us not to stop them from doing. But she looked like she knew she had been stupid, and I had to know. "What happened?"

She looked up at me, clearly anticipating a negative reaction. "I got a note in my feed, through the social profile I had when we were working here. Someone working for Tlacey—a friend—said he had copies of the files and he'd give them to us." She forwarded the message to my feed.

I checked it carefully. The meeting time was set for the next cycle.

I felt this would be the point where a human would sigh, so I sighed.

Tapan said, "I know it could be a trap, but, maybe it isn't? I know him, he's not the greatest guy, but he hates Tlacey." She hesitated. "Will you help me? Please? I'll understand if you say no. I know I've been . . . I know this could be a really bad idea."

I had forgotten that I had a choice, that I wasn't obligated to do what she wanted just because she was here.

Being asked to stay, with a please and an option for refusal, hit me almost as hard as a human asking for my opinion and actually listening to me. I sighed again. I was having a lot of opportunities to do it and I think I was getting good at it. "I'll help you. Right now we need to find a place to get out of sight."

Tapan had a hard currency card from the transit ring, which wasn't tied to any RaviHyral account and so was not traceable. At least, that's what she thought and I hoped she was right. I had never been given any education modules on financial systems and since our modules were crap anyway, I'm not sure that would have helped. ART ran a search for me and the results were mixed. Hard currency cards could be traced, but usually only by non-corporate political or corporate entities. I decided it was probably all right to use it. If the message wasn't a trap, Tlacey must think my clients were back on the transit ring by now. If it was a trap, they would know they could grab us when we walked into the meeting so there was no point in looking for us earlier.

Tapan used the card to pay for a transient room in the block next to the port. While she ran the card through the vending kiosk and got our room assignment, I stood behind her and surveyed the area. The transient rooms were in a narrow warren of corridors, as unlike the main hotel as a real cargo transport was unlike ART. There was no SecSystem to get control of and only one camera at the entrance. I deleted us out of its memory, but I still felt like we—or I—might have been observed at some point. It might just be inherent rogue-SecUnit-on-the-run paranoia.

Tapan led the way to our room. There were other humans hanging around the dimly lit corridors and some looked like they might try to approach her, then saw me and changed their minds. I was bigger than they were, and without cameras it was still hard to control my expression.

ART said, *Tell the human not to touch any surfaces. There may be disease vectors present.*

On the way here I had shared the recording of what I had found at Ganaka Pit. ART said, *This is good news. You were not at fault.* I agreed, sort of. I had been expecting to feel better about it. I mostly just felt awful.

Once inside the room with the door secured, I saw Tapan's shoulders relax and she took a deep breath. The room was just a square box with pads stored in a cabinet for sitting or sleeping, and a small display surface. No cameras, no audio surveillance. There was a tiny attached bath, with a waste-reclaimer and a shower. At least it had a door. I was going to have to pretend to use it at least twice. Yes, that would be the cap on all the fun I was having today. I created a schedule and set an alarm to remind myself to do it.

Tapan dropped her bag on the floor and faced me. "I know you're mad."

I tried to moderate my expression. "I'm not mad." I was furious. I thought my clients were safe, I was free to worry about my own problems, and now I had a tiny human to look after that I couldn't possibly abandon.

She nodded and pushed her braids back. "I know—I mean—I'm sure Rami and Maro were furious. But it's not like I'm not afraid, so that's good."

In my feed, ART said, *What?*

I have no idea, I told it. I said to Tapan, "How is that good?"

She explained, "In the creche, our moms always said that fear was an artificial condition. It's imposed from the outside. So it's possible to fight it. You should do the things you're afraid of."

If a bot with a brain the size of a transport could roll its eyes, that was what ART was doing. I said, "That isn't the purpose of fear." They didn't give us an education module on human evolution, but I had looked it up in the

HubSystem knowledge bases I'd had access to, in an effort to figure out what the hell was going on with humans. It hadn't helped.

She said, "I know, it's supposed to be inspirational." She looked around and went to the cabinet with the seating pads. She pulled them out, sniffed them suspiciously, then took an aerosol capsule out of a pocket on her pack and sprayed them down. "I forgot to ask, did you get a chance to do the research you wanted to do here?"

"Yes. It was . . . inconclusive." It had been damningly conclusive, it just hadn't had the revelatory effect I had been, stupidly, hoping for. I helped her pull the rest of the pads out.

We got them arranged on the floor and sat down. She looked at me and bit her lip. "You're really augmented, aren't you. Like, a lot. Like more than someone would choose voluntarily."

It wasn't a question. I said, "Um, yes."

She nodded. "Was it an accident?"

I realized I had my arms wrapped around myself and was leaning over like I was trying to go into a fetal position. I don't know why this was so stressful. Tapan wasn't afraid of me. I had no reason to be afraid of her. Maybe it was being here again, seeing Ganaka Pit again. Some part of my organic systems remembered what had happened there. In the feed, ART started to play the soundtrack to *Sanctuary Moon* and weirdly, that helped. I said, "I got caught in an explosion. There's not much of me that's human, actually."

Both those statements are true.

She stirred a little, as if debating what to say, then nodded again. "I'm sorry I got you into this. I know you know what you're doing, but . . . I have to try, I have to see if this guy really has our files. Just this once, and then I'll go back to the transit ring."

In my feed, ART turned down the soundtrack to say, *Young humans can be impulsive. The trick is keeping them around long enough to become old humans. This is what my crew tells me and my own observations seem to confirm it.*

I couldn't argue with the wisdom dispensed by ART's absent crew. I remembered humans had needs and asked Tapan, "Did you eat?"

She had bought some meal packs with the hard currency card and had them stuffed in her bag. She offered me one and I told her my augments required me to have a special diet and it wasn't time for me to eat yet. She accepted that readily. Humans apparently don't like to discuss catastrophic injuries to digestive systems, so I didn't need any of the corroborating detail ART had just researched for me. I asked her if she liked media and she said yes, so I sent some files to the display surface in the room, and we watched the first three episodes of *Worldhoppers*. ART was pleased, and I could feel it sitting in my feed, comparing Tapan's reactions to the show to mine.

When Tapan said she wanted to try to sleep, I shut down the display. She curled up on her pad and I lay down on mine and continued watching in the feed with ART.

Two hours and forty-three minutes later, I caught a ping from right outside the door.

I sat up so abruptly, Tapan woke with a start. I motioned for her to be quiet, and she subsided back on the pad, curling around her pack, looking worried. I stood and went to the door, listening. I couldn't hear any breathing, but there was a change in the background noise that told me there was something solid on the other side of the metal door. Cautiously, I did a limited scan.

Yes, there was something out there, but no sign of weapons. I checked the ping and saw it had the same signature as the ping I had caught in the public area during the meeting with Tlacey.

The sexbot was standing on the other side of the door.

It couldn't have been following me all this time. It could have been watching for me on the security cameras, tracking me sporadically through the port when I came back within range. That was not a comforting thought.

It had to belong to Tlacey. If it had been watching me, it would have missed Tapan's unexpected exit from the private shuttle but would have seen her again when we met up at the main hotel or on the way here. Damn it.

But now I knew that. If it hadn't pinged me, I wouldn't have realized it was in play. *Why is it here?* I asked ART.

I assume that's a rhetorical question, it said.

There was only one way to find out. I acknowledged the ping.

The moment stretched. Then it reached out to my feed. It was cautious, the connection almost tentative. It said, *I know what you are. Who sent you?*

I replied, *I'm on contract to a private individual. Why are you communicating with me?*

SecUnits on the same contract don't talk, either verbally or on the feed, unless they absolutely have to in order to perform their duties. Communicating with units on different contracts has to be done through the controlling HubSystems. And SecUnits don't interact with ComfortUnits anyway. Could this be a rogue sexbot? If it was rogue, why was it here on RaviHyral? I didn't know why anybody would stay here voluntarily, including the humans. No, it made more sense if Tlacey owned its contract, and had sent it here to kill Tapan.

If it tried to attack my client, I would tear it apart.

Tapan, sitting on the pad and watching me worriedly, mouthed the words, "What is it?"

I opened a secure channel to her and said, *Someone is outside the door. I'm not sure why.*

That was mostly true. I didn't want to tell Tapan what it was, since that seemed to lead directly to me telling her what I was, which I didn't want to do. Though if I had to destroy it in front of her, I was going to have a lot of explaining to do.

The sexbot replied, *This is you,* and sent me a copy of a public newsburst.

It was from the station, from Port FreeCommerce. This time the headline was "Authorities Admit a SecUnit Unsecured and Location Unknown."

Uh-oh, ART said.

I closed the story by reflex, like that would make it not exist. After three seconds of shock, I made myself open it again.

"Unsecured" is what they call rogue SecUnits when they want humans to listen and not just start screaming. It meant that the knowledge that I had hacked my governor module was no longer confined to me and the members of PreservationAux. They must have been at the stage where everyone in the two survey groups who had survived was being interviewed, and they would have had to guarantee bonds to assert they were telling the truth.

So the company knew now that I had hacked my governor module. That was terrifying, even though I had expected it. It was one of the reasons Mensah had made sure to get me off inventory and out of the deployment center as soon as I came out of repair and reconstruction mode.

Expecting it and having it happen were two different things, something I learned the first time I got shot to pieces.

I skimmed the story in dread and then read it again, closely. The solicitors for several sides in the ongoing legal and civil battles had asked Preservation to produce the SecUnit who had recorded all the damning evidence against GrayCris. This was unusual. It's not like SecUnits can testify in courts. Our recordings are admissible, just like recordings from a drone or security camera or any other inert device, but it's not like we're supposed to have opinions or a perspective on what we record.

After some back and forth, Mensah's solicitor had admitted that she had lost track of me. They phrased it as "released on my own recognizance, as constructs are considered legal sentients under Preservation law," but the journalists hadn't been fooled by that, either. There were a lot of sidebar links to attached articles about constructs, about SecUnits, about rogue SecUnits. There was no mention that this particular unit had had a little problem with murdering the clients supposedly under its protection before, but I had the feeling the company had probably already destroyed any records relating to Ganaka Pit so they couldn't be produced under court injunction.

Tapan whispered, "Are you talking to them, the person?"

"Yes," I told her. To the sexbot, I said, *That's an interesting story but it has nothing to do with me.*

It said, *It's you. Who sent you?*

I said, *That's a story about a dangerous rogue SecUnit. No one would send it anywhere.*

I'm not asking because I want to report you. I won't tell anyone. I'm asking—There's no human controlling you? You're free?

I could feel ART in my feed, carefully extending itself out toward the sexbot.

I have a client, I told it. I had to distract it, if ART was going to be able to get any info. Even though it was a sexbot, it was still a construct, still a whole different proposition from a pilot bot. *Who sent you here? Was it Tlacey?*

Yes. She is my client.

As a ComfortUnit, not a SecUnit. Sending a ComfortUnit into this situation was morally irresponsible and a clear violation of contract. I'm guessing the sexbot knew that.

ART said, *It's not rogue. Its governor module is engaged. So it's probably telling the truth.*

I asked ART, *Can you hack it from here?*

There was a half-second pause while ART explored the idea. ART answered, *No, I can't secure the connection here. It could stop me by cutting off its feed.*

I told the sexbot, *Your client wants to kill my client.*

It didn't reply.

I said, *You told Tlacey about me.* It must have recognized what I was during that first meeting. If it hadn't been sure, seeing the damage I had done to the three humans Tlacey had sent would have been all the confirmation it needed. I was seething, but I kept it out of the feed. As I told ART, bots and constructs can't trust each other, so I don't know why it made me angry. I wish being a construct made me less irrational than the average human but you may have noticed this is not the case. I said, *Your client sent a ComfortUnit to do a SecUnit's job.*

It countered, *She didn't know she needed a SecUnit until today.* It added, *I told her you were a SecUnit, I didn't tell her you were a rogue.*

I wondered if I could believe that. And I wondered if it had tried to explain to Tlacey the impossibility of this assignment. *What do you propose to do?*

There was a pause. A long one, five seconds. *We could kill them.*

Well, that was an unusual approach to its dilemma. *Kill who? Tlacey?*

All of them. The humans here.

I leaned against the wall. If I had been human, I would have rolled my eyes. Though if I had been human, I might have been stupid enough to think it was a good idea.

I also wondered if it knew a lot more about me than what little was in the newsburst.

Picking up on my reaction, ART said, *What does it want?*

To kill all the humans, I answered.

I could feel ART metaphorically clutch its function. If there were no humans, there would be no crew to protect and no reason to do research and fill its databases. It said, *That is irrational.*

I know, I said, *if the humans were dead, who would make the media?* It was so outrageous, it sounded like something a human would say.

Huh.

I said to the sexbot, *Is that how Tlacey thinks constructs talk to each other?*

There was another pause, only two seconds this time. *Yes.* Then, *Tlacey believes you stayed behind to steal the files for the tech group. What did you do for so long in the feed blackout area?*

I was hiding. I know, not my best lie. *Does Tlacey know you want to kill her?* Because the "kill all humans" thing might have come from Tlacey, but the intensity under it was real, and I didn't think it was directed at all humans.

She knows, it said. Then *I didn't tell her about your cli-*

ent, she thinks they all left on the shuttle. She only wanted me to follow you.

A code bundle came through the feed. You can't infect a construct with malware like that, not without sending it through a Sec or HubSystem. Even then I would have to apply it, and without direct orders and a working governor module, there's no way to force me to do it. The only way that code can be applied without my assistance is through a combat override module via my dataport.

It might be killware, but I was not a simple pilot bot, and it would mostly just annoy the hell out of me. Maybe to the point where I tore a door off the wall and ripped the head off a ComfortUnit.

I could just delete the bundle, but I wanted to know what it was so I knew how furious to get. It was small enough for a human's interface to handle, so I shunted it aside to Tapan. I said aloud, "I need you to isolate that for me. Don't open it yet."

She signaled assent through the feed and pulled the bundle into her temp storage. The other thing about killware and malware is that they can't do anything to humans or augmented humans.

The sexbot hadn't said anything else and I sent a ping in time to feel it withdraw its feed. It was walking away down the corridor.

I waited until I was sure, then stepped back from the

door. I debated staying here, or moving Tapan. Now that I knew something was hacking the security cameras to watch me, I could use countermeasures. I probably should have been doing that from the beginning, but you may have noticed that for a terrifying murderbot I fuck up a lot.

"It's gone," I told Tapan. "Can you check out that code bundle for me?"

She got that inward look that humans have when they're deep in their feed. After a minute, she said, "It's malware. Pretty standard... Maybe they thought it would get your augments, but that's kind of amateurish for Tlacey. Hold it. There's a message string in here, attached to the code."

ART and I waited. Tapan's face did something complicated, settling on worry. "This is weird." She turned to the display surface and made the completely unnecessary gesture that some humans can't help doing when they send something from their feed to display.

It was the message string, three words. *Please help me.*

I moved us to a different room, near an emergency exit, in another section of the hostel. The sexbot might be alert for hacking, so I removed the access plate, manually broke the lock, and replaced the plate again while Tapan watched the corridor. Once we were inside, I told Tapan some of what the sexbot had said, mostly the part about how it claimed Tlacey didn't know Tapan was here. (I didn't tell her our visitor had been a sexbot because Tlacey had figured out what I was and didn't want to waste any more human bodyguards on me.) "But we don't know that that's true, or that this operative won't tell Tlacey you're here now."

Tapan looked confused. "But why did they tell you anything?"

That was a good question. "I don't know. They don't like Tlacey, but that might not be the only reason."

Tapan bit her lip, considering. "I think I should still try to keep the meeting. It's only four hours from now."

I'm used to humans wanting to do things that can get them killed. Maybe too used to it. I knew we should leave now. But I needed time to hack enough of the security system to get past the sexbot. Once I did that, it seemed wrong not to wait the short time to make the meeting, which Tapan was reasonably sure Tlacey didn't know about. Reasonably sure.

It was probably a trap.

I needed to think. I told Tapan I was going to sleep for a while and laid down on my side on my section of padding. My recharge cycle isn't obvious but it doesn't look like a human sleeping, so what I was actually going to do was play some media in the background of my feed while I worked on my security countermeasures and looked up my old module on risk assessment.

Thirty-two minutes later, I heard movement. I thought Tapan was getting up to go to the restroom facility, but then she settled on the pads behind me, not quite touching my back. I had set my breathing to sound deep and even, like a human sleeping, with occasional random variations to add verisimilitude, so the fact that I had frozen in place wasn't obvious.

I had never had a human touch me, or almost touch me, like this before and it was deeply, deeply weird.

Calm down, ART said, not helpfully.

I was too frozen to respond. After three seconds, ART added, *She's frightened. You are a reassuring presence.*

I was still too frozen to answer ART, but I upped my body heat. Over the next two hours, she yawned twice, breathed deeply, and snorted occasionally. At the end of that time I changed my breathing and moved a little, and she immediately slid off my pad and over to hers.

By that time, I had a plan, sort of.

I convinced Tapan that I should go to the meeting, and she should get on a public shuttle to the transit ring immediately. She was reluctant. "I don't want to abandon you," she said. "You're only involved in this because of us."

That hit home so hard my insides clenched. I had to lean over and pretend to look through my bag to hide my expression. Company emergency protocol allows clients to abandon their SecUnits if necessary, even in situations where the company might never be able to retrieve them. Tapan was making me think of Mensah, yelling that she wouldn't leave me. I said, "It'll help me the most if you go back to the transit ring."

It took a while, but I finally convinced her this was for the best for both of us.

Tapan left the hostel first, wearing both extra jackets from her pack to change her body shape and with the hood of one pulled up to conceal her hair and shadow her face. (This was mostly to make her feel more confident, and because I didn't want to explain the extent to which I could gain temporary control over portions of Ravi-Hyral's admittedly not-great security system.) I watched her on the security cameras until I saw her reach the public dock about one hundred meters away, go down the walkway to the embarkation area, then board the shuttle that was scheduled to leave in twenty-one minutes. ART sent me an acknowledgment as it slid into the shuttle's controls to guard the bot pilot again. Then I left the hostel.

I'd prepared a hack for the security cameras that was much more sophisticated than the one I'd been using up to this point. It involved getting into the operational code and setting the system on a tenth of a second delay, then deleting Tapan out and randomly replacing that part of the recording with pieces cut from earlier. This would work because the sexbot would be scanning the recordings the same way I would, using a body configuration scan. I didn't match SecUnit standard anymore, but the sexbot had had plenty of time to scan my new configuration during that first meeting with Tlacey.

Right now I wanted the sexbot's attention on me, and not the public dock. I let the cameras track me out of the port and back toward the tube access. Then I started the hack.

I was only 97 percent certain this meeting was a trap.

Chapter Eight

WHEN I REACHED THE small food service counter in the contractor district, a human was there who matched the image Tapan had sent to my feed. As I sat down at the table he looked up at me, his expression nervous, sweat beading on his pale forehead. I said, "Tapan couldn't come," and sent his feed the brief recording Tapan had made with her interface. It was her standing next to me in the room at the hostel, holding my arm and explaining that the files could be given to me. Wow, I looked uncomfortable.

His gaze went inward as he reviewed the recording, then his body relaxed a little. He slid a memory clip over to me. I took it and checked the cameras.

Nothing. No potential threats, no one showing interest in us. The counter served drinks with a lot of bubbles in them and fried protein in the shape of water fauna and flora. Everyone else was busy eating or talking. There was no one suspicious in the corridor or mall area outside, no one watching, no one waiting.

This was not a trap.

The human said uncertainly, "Should we order something? To make it look like we're not—you know?"

I told him, "No one's watching, you can leave," and pushed to my feet. I had to get back to the port.

If this wasn't a trap, the real trap was somewhere else.

On the way back to the dock, I checked the schedule. The shuttle was now listed as delayed.

As I reached the embarkation area, I was reviewing the security recording from the time Tapan had boarded the shuttle. On visual, I spotted the sexbot coming toward me from the far end of the walkway.

I had gotten to the point in the recording where two humans with Port Authority identification had stopped the shuttle's departure and removed Tapan. ART slid out of the shuttle and back into my feed. It said, *If I had my armed drones, this would be easier.*

When the sexbot reached me, I said, "Where is she?"

"In Tlacey's private shuttle. I'll show you."

I followed it along the walkway, then down the ramp that split off toward the private shuttle docks. ART said, *Why is it showing you where your human is?*

I said, *Because Tlacey doesn't want Tapan, she wants me.*

ART was quiet as we went past the private shuttle

slots toward the bigger, more expensive section at the end. Then it said, *Retrieve your human and make Tlacey regret this.*

We stopped in front of the access to a shuttle hatch. No one was outside, and most of the activity was down toward the other end of the docks. The sexbot turned to face me.

It opened its hand, and I recognized the small object. It was a combat override module. It said, "They won't allow you aboard unless you let me install this."

In my feed, ART said, *Ah.*

They wanted us in the shuttle so that they could dispose of the bodies. Or Tapan's body. Me they obviously intended to keep.

A combat override module contains code that will take over my system, overriding the governor module and the company factory-set protocols, and placing me under the direct verbal or comm control of whoever the module designates. This was how GrayCris took over DeltFall's SecUnits, and tried to take over me.

I said, "If I accept that, will they release my client?"

In the feed the sexbot whispered, *You know they won't.* Aloud, it said, "Yes."

I turned and let it insert the module into my data port. (The data port that ART had disconnected when it altered my configuration. With my governor module hacked, it had been the only way left to assert control over me, so disabling it had been a priority.)

The module clicked into place and I had a moment of purely irrational fear. ART must have picked up on it because it said, *Please, my MedSystem makes no mistakes.* Nothing happened, and from the security camera I had control of, I saw that I managed to keep the relief out of my expression.

The sexbot's expression was Unit standard neutral, and I followed it into the shuttle. A human stood just inside the lock, armed, his eyes flicking nervously between me and the sexbot. He said, "Is it under control?"

"Yes," the sexbot said.

He stepped back and his jaw moved as he spoke in his feed. I couldn't hack anything without the sexbot knowing, so I waited. I kept my expression blank. I had no way of knowing what the combat override module was supposed to make me do, but I was assuming it would put me under Tlacey's control. I suspected the humans, and the sexbot, weren't sure what the outward effect would be.

Once we were through the lock, it cycled shut and a launch warning went through the feed, ending in an audible beep from the comm system. Tlacey must have bribed someone for immediate clearance, because there was a clunk as the lock disengaged and then the shuttle slid out of its slot.

I have you on my scan, ART said.

The human led the way through the shuttle. It was a large model, and the access corridor went past hatchways to cabins and the engineering section before ending in a big compartment. There was cushioned bench seating against the walls and acceleration chairs to the front, near the hatch that must lead to the forward part of the ship. There were six unknown humans in the room, four armed and two unarmed crew. One of the armed humans held Tapan by the shoulder and had a projectile weapon pressed to her head.

Tlacey stood up from a chair and looked me over with a smile. She said, "Take little Tapan to a cabin. I'll want to talk to her later about her work."

Tapan's eyes were wide and frightened. I kept my expression blank. She tried to say, "Eden, I'm sorry! I'm sorry—" but the guard pulled her through another hatchway and down a corridor. I didn't react, since I wanted her out of the line of fire. I listened for the hatch to close, then focused on Tlacey.

She strolled toward me, thoughtful now. I guess the triumphant smile had been for Tapan's benefit. The two other unarmed humans were watching with nervous curiosity, the armed guards still looked cautious. To the sexbot, Tlacey said, "You really think this is one of the units from the Ganaka Pit accident?"

The sexbot started to reply, and I said, "But we all know that wasn't an accident, don't we."

Now I had everybody's attention.

I kept my gaze straight ahead, a good SecUnit still under the control of the combat override module. Tlacey stared at me, then her eyes narrowed. "Who am I talking to?"

That was almost funny. "You think I'm a puppet? You know that's not the way we work."

Tlacey was beginning to be afraid. "Who sent you?"

I lowered my head to meet her gaze. "I came for my client."

Tlacey's jaw moved as she gave a command in the feed, and the sexbot started to shift sideways into a combat position.

ART said, *The shuttle is clear of the port and moving into an orbit around the moon. Do you have a moment to let me in?*

I said, *Be fast,* and let ART in. I had the sensation again, my head shoved underwater, being temporarily incapacitated as ART used me as a bridge to reach the bot controlling the shuttle.

It was quick, but the sexbot had time to punch me in the jaw. Tlacey must have ordered that; it wasn't the way a unit would attack another unit. It hurt, but only in the way that would piss me off. When I didn't react immediately, Tlacey relaxed and grinned. "I like a mouthy bot. This is going to be interesting—"

ART was in the shuttle's systems and I was clear. I caught the sexbot's arm and flung it across the room toward the three armed guards. One went down, one stumbled into a chair, the third started to lift his weapon. I knocked Tlacey out of my way and stepped on the sexbot as I went over it, thumping it back down to the deck. I grabbed the muzzle of the energy weapon and shoved it upright just as he fired. The discharge struck the curved ceiling. I ripped it out of his grasp, dislocating his shoulder and at least three fingers, and slammed his head down on the console.

The guard who had already fallen to the deck had a projectile weapon and I felt two impacts, one to my side and one to my thigh. Now that's the kind of attack that actually hurts. I extended my right arm and fired my inbuilt energy weapon, catching him with two bolts in the chest. I stepped sideways to avoid an energy weapon blast from the guard who had fallen into the chair, and my third shot hit him in the shoulder. I had the blasts set to narrow, and they created deep burn wounds that usually incapacitated humans rapidly with shock and pain and, you know, having holes burned into their chest cavities.

I pivoted and threw the captured gun as a distraction.

The first unarmed human was on the deck, a smoking wound in her back; the guard who had missed me had shot her. The second flung herself across the compartment to try to grab a fallen projectile weapon, so I shot her in the shoulder and the leg.

The sexbot rolled to its feet and charged me, I caught it, went down on my back, and flung it off and over my head. I twisted around and up to my knees but couldn't get all the way up due to the wound in my right thigh. The sexbot shoved upright and I grabbed its leg and popped the knee out of the socket. It went down and I took out its left shoulder joint. Slamming it down to the deck, I turned to see Tlacey reaching for one of the fallen weapons. I said, "Touch that weapon and I'll take it away from you and insert it into your rib cage."

She froze. She was panting from fear, eyes staring. I said, "Tell your sexbot to stop fighting."

It was still struggling to get up and it was just going to hurt itself further. Especially if it made me mad again.

Tlacey straightened slowly, her jaw working, and the sexbot relaxed. I said, *ART, cut off Tlacey's feed.*

Done, ART said.

Tlacey winced as her feed went down. I told Tlacey, "Give the sexbot a verbal command to obey me until further notice. Try to give it any other command and I'll rip your tongue out."

Tlacey huffed out a breath, then said, "Unit, obey the crazy rogue SecUnit until further notice." To me, she said, "You need to get better threats."

I put a hand on the nearest chair seat and shoved myself to my feet. "I don't make threats, I'm just telling you what I'm going to do."

Her jaw hardened. Two of the humans in the room had stopped breathing, the unarmed one that the guard had shot while aiming for me and the first one I had shot. Tlacey hadn't noticed.

I looked down at the sexbot, which looked up at me. "Stay down," I said.

It sent me an acknowledgment. I stepped over it, grabbed Tlacey's arm, and dragged her down the corridor to the cabin where her guard had taken Tapan.

She said quickly, "So you're a free agent, right? I can give you a job. Whatever you want—"

I thought, *You don't have anything I want.* I said, "All you had to do was give them the fucking files and none of us would be in this situation."

The look she threw back at me was startled, incredulous. I didn't sound like her idea of a SecUnit, rogue or otherwise, I guess.

Humans should really do more research. There were operating manuals that would have warned her not to fuck with us.

Tlacey stopped at a closed hatch, said, "Bassom, it's me," and hit the release. The door slid up.

Tapan was half sprawled across the bunk on the far wall, blood spreading across the flower pattern on her T-shirt, drops of it splashed on the brown skin of the bare arm pressed against the wound in her side. Her raspy breath sounded loud in the small cabin. The bodyguard stared at us, eyes wide.

"He panicked when he heard the shots," Tlacey gasped. "You can't—"

Oh yeah, I could.

I swung Tlacey to shield me as the bodyguard brought up his weapon. Multiple shots hit her back but I'd already crushed her windpipe. I took another projectile in the chest as I crossed the cabin, threw him against the wall, jammed my arm up under his chin, and triggered my energy weapon.

I stepped back and let his body drop.

I turned away from it and leaned over Tapan. I said, stupidly, "It's me." Her eyes were shut and she was breathing through gritted teeth. I clamped my hand over the wound to stop the bleeding and said, *ART, help.*

ART said, *I've been guiding the shuttle toward the transit ring, where I can dock it with myself. ETA is seventeen minutes. MedSystem is prepping for your arrival.*

I sank down beside Tapan. She was just conscious

enough to reach over and squeeze my hand. I pulled the useless combat override module out of the back of my neck and tossed it away.

I had made a huge mistake, which seemed blindingly obvious in hindsight. I had known the invitation to exchange the signing bonus for the files was a trap from the beginning and I should have convinced Rami and the others not to return to RaviHyral. The augmented human security consultant I was pretending to be would have done that. I was used to taking orders from humans and trying to mitigate whatever damage their stupid ideas did to them, but I had wanted to work with a group again, I had enjoyed how they had listened to me, I had put my need to get to RaviHyral above the safety of my clients.

I was just as shit at being a security consultant as any human.

Chapter Nine

BY THE TIME WE were on approach to the transit ring, ART had cleared us with the ring's Port Authority. Shuttles weren't supposed to be able to dock with transports without advance notice, but ART took care of approach permission, and forged its captain's feed signature to pay the fine for not giving prior notice of the scheduled trip. They didn't suspect anything; nobody knew transports could have bots sophisticated enough to fake being human in the feed. I sure hadn't known it.

The locks weren't compatible but ART solved that problem by pulling the shuttle into an empty module meant for lab space. It sat us down, filled the module with atmosphere, and then cycled our lock. I got upright and carried Tapan out and up the access into the main section. ComfortUnit followed me.

The MedSystem was ready by the time I walked in and laid Tapan down on the platform. Drones whizzed around me and I picked up the MedSystem feed's instruction to remove her shoes and clothes. As the cradle closed around her, I sank down beside the platform.

She was out now, the MedSystem keeping her under while it finished its assessment and started to work. Two medical drones flew around me, one diving in toward my shoulder and the other poking at the wound in my thigh. I ignored them.

A larger drone flew in, carrying Tapan's bag, her bloodstained jacket, and my knapsack. ART flashed me a view of the other drones still inside the shuttle. Four of the humans in the shuttle were still alive, though unconscious. ART had sent drones to scrub and sterilize away my fluids and Tapan's blood from the shuttle's interior. ART had already wiped the bot pilot's memory and deleted any security data. It was also chatting casually with transit ring launch authority with a forged feed signature from one of the dead humans.

I watched as the drones finished and retreated, then ART sealed the shuttle again and launched it with a filed flight plan back to RaviHyral. The onboard bot pilot would land it, full of terribly injured humans, and no one would know they hadn't done it to each other until they were all conscious and told their stories. Though maybe some wouldn't want to tell the story of how they had helped kidnap another human. Whatever happened, it would give us all time to get out of here.

I asked ART, *How did you know to do that?* though I already knew the answer.

It knew I knew, but it said, *Episode 179 of* The Rise and Fall of Sanctuary Moon.

ComfortUnit knelt beside me. "Can I help?"

"No." The medical drones were clamped onto me now, digging for the projectiles, and I was leaking onto ART's pristine MedSystem floor. The anesthetic was making me numb. "How did you know I was one of the Ganaka Pit units?"

It said, "I saw you get off the tube access in that section. There's nothing else down there. It's not in the historical database anymore, but the humans still tell each other horror stories about it. If you were really a rogue and not under orders to go there, then there was an eighty-six percent chance that you went there because you were one of the units involved."

I believed it. "Drop your wall."

It did, and I rode the feed into its brain. I could feel ART with me, alert for traps. But I found the governor module, rendered it null, and slid back out into my own body again.

The ComfortUnit had fallen back, sitting down on the deck with a thump, staring at me.

I said, "Go away. Don't let me see you again. Don't hurt anyone on this transit ring or I'll find you."

It shoved upright, unsteady. More of ART's drones flicked through the air, making sure it didn't try to damage anything, herding it toward the door. It followed the drones out into the corridor. Through ART's feed I watched it go through to the main hatch, where the lock cycled and it went out into the transit ring.

ART watched it walk away through its lock camera. It said, *I thought you might destroy it.*

Too tired and numb to talk, I signaled a negative through the feed. It hadn't had a choice. And I hadn't broken its governor module for its sake. I did it for the four ComfortUnits at Ganaka Pit who had no orders and no directive to act and had voluntarily walked into the meat grinder to try to save me and everyone else left alive in the installation.

ART said, *Now get on the other platform. The shuttle will land soon and there is a great deal of evidence to destroy.*

When Tapan woke, I was sitting on the MedSystem's platform holding her hand. The MedSystem had taken care of my wounds, and I'd cleaned off all the blood. The projectiles that had hit me and the energy bursts from my own weapons had left holes in my clothes, and ART had produced a new set for me from its recycler. It was basically ART's crew uniform without the logos: pants with lots of sealable pockets, a long-sleeved shirt with a collar just high enough to cover my data port, and a soft hooded jacket, all of it either dark blue or black. I fed my bloody clothes into the recycler so the waste-reclamation levels would be neutral and ART wouldn't have to forge its log.

Tapan blinked up at me, confused. "Um," she said, and squeezed my hand. The drugs made her expression bleary. "What happened?"

I said, "They tried to kill us again. We had to leave. We're back on the transit ring, on my friend's ship."

Her eyes widened as she remembered. She winced, and muttered, "Fuckers."

"Your friend was telling the truth, he gave me your files." I held up the memory clip, and showed her I was putting it into the interface pocket in her bag. I'd checked it already for malware or tracers. "This ship has to leave soon. I need you to call Rami and Maro to come meet us outside the embarkation zone."

"Okay." She fumbled at her ear, and I handed her the blue feed interface. One of ART's drones had found it in Tlacey's pocket. She took it, started to put it back in her ear, and hesitated. "They're going to be so mad."

"Yeah, they are." I thought they would be so glad to have her alive it wouldn't occur to them to be angry.

She winced again. "I'm sorry. I should have listened to you."

"It wasn't your fault."

Her brow crinkled. "I kind of think it was."

"It was my fault."

"It's both our faults then, but we won't tell anybody," Tapan decided, and wiggled the interface into her ear.

I did a quick walk-through of the areas of the ship I had used, to make sure nothing was out of place. ART's drones had already come through, taking Tapan's bloody clothes to be cleaned and sterilizing surfaces so any attempt to collect trace evidence would fail. Not that ART intended to be here when the investigation started. We were all leaving immediately, but ART believed in contingency plans. I started to remove the comm interface ART had given me. "You need to clean this, too."

No, ART said. *Keep it. Maybe we'll come within range of each other again.*

The MedSystem had already sterilized itself and deleted the records of my configuration change and the emergency trauma treatments to both me and Tapan. I was waiting for her when she came out of the bath facility. Drones followed her in to clean away any traces of her presence, and she said, "I'm ready." She had stuffed her old clothes into her pack and was wearing fresh ones. She still looked a little bleary.

We walked out together and the lock sealed behind us. I had the cameras in the embarkation zone and ART was already doctoring the security recordings on its lock to erase our presence.

We met Rami, Maro, and the rest of their group at a food stand outside the embarkation zone. Rami had messaged me that they had already bought passage on a passenger transport leaving within the hour. They greeted Tapan enthusiastically, with tears and admonishments to each other not to squeeze her too hard.

I'd told them already not to talk about it in public. Rami turned and handed me a hard currency card. "Your friend Art said this was a good way to pay you."

"Right." I took it and tucked it in a sealable pocket.

They were all watching me now and it was a little nerve-racking. Rami said, "So, you're going?"

I had my eye on a cargo transport heading the right direction. With luck I should be leaving within minutes of their departure. "Yes, I should hurry."

"Can we hug you?" Maro let go of Tapan and faced me.

"Uh." I didn't step back, but it must have been obvious the answer was no.

Maro nodded. "Okay. This is for you." She wrapped her arms around herself and squeezed.

I said, "I've got to go," and walked away down the mall.

Fading, already disengaging from its lock, ART said in my feed, *Be careful. Find your crew.*

I tapped the feed in acknowledgment, because if I tried to say anything else I was going to sound stupid and emotional.

I didn't know what I was going to do now, if I was going to go ahead with my plan or not. I had hoped finding out what had happened at Ganaka Pit would clear everything up, but maybe revelations like that only happened in the media.

Speaking of which, I needed to grab some more downloads before my next transport left. It was going to be a long trip.

About the Author

MARTHA WELLS has written many fantasy novels, including *The Wizard Hunters, Wheel of the Infinite,* the Books of the Raksura series (beginning with *The Cloud Roads*), and the Nebula-nominated *The Death of the Necromancer,* as well as YA fantasy novels, short stories, and nonfiction. She has had stories in *Black Gate, Realms of Fantasy, Stargate Magazine, Lightspeed Magazine,* and in the anthologies *Elemental, Tales of the Emerald Serpent, The Other Half of the Sky, The Gods of H. P. Lovecraft,* and *MECH: Age of Steel*. She has also written media tie-ins for *Stargate: Atlantis* and most recently *Star Wars: Razor's Edge*. The last book in the Books of the Raksura series, *The Harbors of the Sun,* was released in July 2017.